AMERICA DOWN
A POST-APOCALYPTIC EMP SURVIVAL THRILLER

KEITH TAYLOR

About the Author

Keith Taylor is the author of the bestselling Last Man Standing series, This Is the Way the World Ends, and now the Willow Falls EMP survival series.

Taylor hails from Manchester in the north of England. He lives with his wife, Otgontsetseg, and spends most of his time in Ulaanbaatar, Mongolia. He's been deported from more than one country, once spent two months living in his car, has crapped in the wilderness everywhere from the Gobi Desert to the Pamir mountains on the Afghan border, and he survives on a diet of meat, cheese, beer and cigarettes. He probably shouldn't still be alive, but for now appears to be unkillable.

Website: **authorkeithtaylor.com**

:::1:::

"LADIES AND GENTLEMEN, the captain has turned off the fasten seat belt sign. You may now feel free to move around the cabin. We anticipate clear skies and a comfortable flight into Norfolk, but as always we recommend that you keep your seat belt securely fastened while seated."

First Officer Benjamin Cole listened to the chief flight attendant's announcement, offering a silent apology for the endless complaints the cabin crew were about to endure.

"Unfortunately," she continued, "due to technical difficulties in Knoxville we will be unable to offer a beverage service on today's flight. We *do* apologize for the inconvenience, and we appreciate your understanding. Thank you for choosing American."

Captain Evan Blackmore fought to hold back a smirk as Cole slumped back in his chair. "She went with 'technical difficulties', huh? She should have just told them the truth. 'Hey, folks, the idiot who drives the catering truck showed up drunk and crashed into a set of service stairs.' It might not be diplomatic, but at least we wouldn't take the heat when the folks back there decide to rant about it on Twitter."

Cole scowled at the captain. "You know we'll never hear the end of this, right? It'll be like Dallas all over again."

Evan reached over to the radio and switched frequencies from the Knoxville tower to Atlanta Center ACC. "What was Dallas? Was that the flight with all the food poisoning?"

"No, that was San Diego. C'mon, I must have told you about Dallas a hundred times. Some joker who'd just been handed his pink slip decided to send us out with nothing but vegan meals on a fourteen hour flight to Beijing. From *Texas*, of all places. Three hundred ninety angry barbecue fans raising hell over cold soybean wraps. Cabin crew wouldn't shut up about it for weeks, as if it was *my* job to arrange the damned catering."

Cole ran his hands over the instruments, performing checks he could do in his sleep after six years on the flight deck. "Just make sure the crew knows this was *your* call, not mine. I'd have been happy to wait a half hour for the next window if it meant we could take on booze and coffee."

Evan smiled and shook his head. "Ben, old buddy, you're just gonna have to take one for the team. If I'm not home to meet the girls by two I might as well just tell Jill's lawyers she can have full custody, know what I'm saying? Once is bad enough, but a second no show in a month? And on July Fourth, of all days? Not happening."

Cole felt his anger begin to subside at the mention of Evan's kids. He knew the captain had been struggling since his divorce, desperately juggling a hectic flight schedule with the demands of a vindictive ex-wife who seemed hellbent on turning her young daughters against their father. It was tough to stay mad at a guy who was just trying to get home to see his little girls.

"Fine, but you owe me one," he reluctantly conceded. "You got any plans for tonight?"

Evan held up a silencing finger as he spoke to air traffic control through his headset. "Ah, we'd prefer two niner zero as a final for today, Atlanta Center. Please confirm… Roger, climbing to two niner zero for American three seven two. Thanks for your help, Center, and happy Fourth." He took the yoke and pulled gently back, nosing the plane up towards its final altitude before replying. "Oh yeah, big plans. I got us a little place out at Virginia Beach for the weekend. You know, one of those AirBnB rentals? S'mores on the beach while we watch the fireworks tonight, then we got the water park, children's museum, Virginia aquarium, the whole works. Gotta squeeze about a month's worth of memories into a long weekend. I'm already exhausted just thinking about it." He shot a sidelong glance at Cole as he leveled off, checked his instruments and flipped on the autopilot. "How about you? Dare I ask?"

Cole pretended to focus on the instrument panel, but he couldn't keep the grin from creeping to his lips. "Plans? Oh, you know me."

Evan barked out a laugh. "Yeah, I know you. What's her name?"

"Katie. Met her last month at a wedding, and we finally managed to get our schedules lined up. No big plans. Might take her out on the boat on Saturday, or maybe we'll just stay in bed if she's game." He sighed and shifted uncomfortably in his chair. "Damn, I gotta go take a leak. You all set here?"

Evan gave his instruments one final check and nodded. "Yeah, go ahead, slugger. No need to call in one of the girls, just be quick about it. Two shakes and zip up."

Cole chuckled as he freed his belt and climbed out of the chair. He didn't need to be told twice to hurry. According to FAA regulations it was a fireable offense to leave a pilot alone on the flight deck, even for a second. Standard procedure was to call in a flight attendant whenever the captain or first officer left to use the restroom or grab a drink, but even under jumpy post-9/11 security the rule was only loosely observed once a plane was in the air. Among pilots trust counted for a hell of a lot. You couldn't fly without it, and after hundreds of hours sharing a cockpit Cole would happily trust Evan with his life.

The flight deck door unlocked with a soft click, and as Cole passed through and pulled it closed behind him he heard the dull thunk of the heavy security latch slide automatically into place behind him. He waited for a moment until the electronic keypad beside the door flashed its little red LED light, confirmation that the door was securely locked, and then turned to face the cabin.

It wasn't until he caught sight of the passengers that Cole remembered the missing drinks service, and he suddenly felt the sort of deer-in-the-headlights frozen horror of a teen who accidentally drops a condom at the feet of his date's disapproving father. A dozen angry scowls shot back at him from the small first class section. It was all he could manage to flash an awkward smile before darting quickly to the safety of the bathroom.

Ha, first class. On this narrow-body 737 the first class cabin was little more than a cruel joke. The folks up front got two inches more leg room, three extra inches for their elbows and a half inch wider fake smile from the flight attendants, but the Atlanta-Norfolk route was far from prestigious, and the twelve year old equipment far from luxurious. The only real benefits of paying twice the price of an economy ticket were the complimentary drinks and the three-ply toilet tissue in the bathroom, and Cole had left these folks with nothing but the fancy butt paper.

As he unzipped and began to pee he could almost *hear* the passengers mentally composing their letters of complaint to the airline. *Dear Sir/Madam, I was deeply disappointed on my recent flight to discover that... yada yada yada, gimme some free miles or I'll start yelling.*

Cole was mid stream and dreading having to face the passengers again when the lights suddenly went out. For a moment the floor shuddered and the strip of lighting around the mirror seemed to glow just a little brighter than usual, as if a little extra power surged through the bulb, and then it flickered out with the pop of a fried filament, plunging him into absolute darkness. In the sudden gloom he heard the sound of his urine stream drift from the center of the bowl to the edge, and then he felt a splash against his legs as it bounced off the lid back in his direction.

"Damn it," he cursed, shaking off and buttoning up clumsily in the coffin darkness before blindly reaching out for the paper towels beside the basin. He knew this bathroom like the back of his hand, but in the total darkness the small, cramped room suddenly felt alien and unfamiliar, as if everything in his world had subtly shifted. His elbows nudged against walls that felt closer than usual, and his fingers pawed around a wash basin that seemed to be just an inch or two to the right of where he remembered it. For the life of him he couldn't find the narrow paper towel slot in the wall.

After struggling for a moment he turned awkwardly in the darkness and pulled open the door a crack, allowing bright sunlight from the cabin to flood into the room. He grabbed a towel, wiped down the front of his pants and washed his hands before stepping out and closing the door behind him. The last thing he wanted to do was face the wrath of the passengers, but before returning to the flight deck he knew he had to make the walk of shame down the aisle to let Samantha, the chief flight attendant, know the lights had blown.

After just a couple of steps he stopped suddenly in his tracks. He cocked his head, frowning as he listened to the hum of the cabin.

Something was wrong.

He couldn't hear the engines.

•▼•

:::2:::

"NAH, YOU'RE OUT of your mind. She's a six and a half. Seven at best. I mean sure, I wouldn't kick her outta bed, but she'd have to be crazy if she thought I'd let her stick around for breakfast. I've had better."

Samantha Bennett concentrated on keeping her sparkling Pan Am smile fixed even as she felt the eyes of the passenger linger on her ass. His buddy in the seat beside him had already made a clumsy effort to press his crotch up against her in the aisle as he was boarding, and she'd smelled the harsh, chemical bite of cheap vodka on their breath the moment they'd stepped off the jetway.

Typical first class newbies. She could tell from their shiny, ill fitting suits and their oh-so-obvious unjustified over-confidence that both of these guys were on their first visit up from cattle class, and suddenly they thought they were big shots. That was the problem with first class. You give a certain type of passenger the slightest taste of the high life and it goes to their head faster than a glass of champagne.

The guy in the aisle seat, the one who claimed he'd 'had better' than Samantha, looked like he'd only started shaving last week. He sat with his legs spread wide, his knee jutting out into the aisle, but he clearly hadn't had the practice to perfect the casual masculine swagger of a real man. He didn't look rakishly confident, the master of his own world. He just looked like a kid who hadn't wiped properly the last time he'd gone to the bathroom.

"Hey, stewardess," he called out, flagging her down like a cab, "can you get me a scotch on the rocks?"

Samantha turned, widening her smile just a little while making it clear with her cold, emotionless eyes that she'd love nothing more than to throw this punk out the window. "I'm sorry, *sir*," she said, somehow resisting the urge to say *asshole*, "but as I said after takeoff I'm afraid we won't be able to offer a beverage service on this flight. If you're thirsty I can bring you bottled water, though I'm afraid we don't have any ice."

The young man shook his head sullenly, and Samantha turned away quickly so she could give her mouth a break. That was the most difficult part of the job. It wasn't the late nights and early mornings, the recycled air, the constant hotel stays or the challenge of walking up and down a plane through turbulence for hours on end. It was forcing a smile for pricks who seemed to think flight attendants were halfway between slave and stripper.

"She's probably a dyke anyway," the guy in the window seat muttered under his breath, unaware that all flight attendants train themselves to hear quiet voices over the sound of the engines from day one on the job.

Idiot.

The cockpit door swung open and the first officer, Ben Cole, stepped out, and as he closed the door behind him Samantha was torn between a fake and a genuine smile. She was mad at the guy. She wanted to make him and the captain suffer for subjecting her to a planeload of passengers who blamed her for the lack of drinks, but on the other hand Cole was... well, he was nice. He'd always treated her kindly, unlike many officers she'd worked with. Most flight crew thought of cabin crew as glorified wait staff, but Cole was one of the good guys, even if he was a bit of a hound dog.

The genuine smile won by a nose, but as the first officer turned to face the cabin he barely seemed to notice her. Instead he focused on the angry faces of the passengers, a haunted look flitting across his face, and he quickly dashed to the safety of the bathroom.

Yeah, that's right. Leave me to deal with the fallout.

"Hey, stewardess." She felt a sharp tug on her sleeve and looked down. *This guy again.* "You sure you don't have any booze at all? Not even for first class? Come on, you gotta have something up there."

Samantha pulled her arm away, backing away from his eye watering vodka breath, and gave him her coldest smile. "I'm very sorry, sir, I'm afraid we really don't have anyth—"

Her voice trailed off as the overhead lights flickered out along the length of the cabin, and beneath her feet she felt an odd vibration. It wasn't turbulence. The opposite, in fact. The vibrations in the cabin floor were so familiar she barely felt them any more, but now it felt as if she were suddenly standing on firm ground. She couldn't quite put her finger on what was wrong. It was almost as if...

The first officer emerged from the bathroom. He started to walk purposefully towards her, then abruptly stopped. He frowned, cocked his head for a moment, and Samantha's heart jumped to her throat as she saw him give her *the look*.

Every flight attendant knew the secret language that allowed flight crew and cabin crew to communicate without alarming passengers. There were dozens of subtle signals that meant everything from 'get the vomit bags ready' to 'warn the Air Marshal about the guy in seat 32C', but only once before in her career had she seen *the look*. It was subtle, a gentle nod with eye contact that lasted just a moment too long for comfort, but to Samantha it couldn't have been clearer if he'd been yelling through a bullhorn.

Something's badly wrong. Come here. Keep your voice down.

She was at Cole's side in a matter of seconds, turning to tug the privacy curtain across the aisle to block the view of the passengers.

"What's going on?" she asked, leaning in and keeping her voice to a whisper.

Cole frowned as he keyed his security code into the keypad beside the door. "We've lost both engines. You don't hear it?"

Samantha concentrated on the sound. Flight attendants trained themselves to tune out the drone of the engines, but as soon as she listened out for it it became obvious. The cabin was still filled with the usual quiet but pervasive wall of sound that accompanies any airplane in flight, but it was missing the low hum of the enormous turbofan engines mounted to each wing.

"Oh my God, both engines?" she whispered, gripping him by the arm. "Are we going to be OK?"

Cole nodded. "Don't worry, we train for this. We just have to... why the hell won't this door unlock?" He keyed in the code for a third time, and as he hit the final number there was silence where he expected the click of the latch disengaging. "Oh, don't tell me..." He reached for the handle and turned it, and his expression turned grim as the latch released and the door began to swing open without resistance.

"What is it? What's wrong?"

Cole ignored her question. "Just go back and keep everyone calm." He tried a reassuring smile, but Samantha could see through it to the fear in his eyes. "Don't worry, we have this under control. Everything will be just fine."

He couldn't have sounded less convincing if he'd tried.

•▼•

∴3∴

COLE NOTICED THE dead instrument panels before anything else. Where usually dozens of bright indicator lights competed with the brightly lit EFIS, the electronic flight instrument system, for the attention of the pilots, now there was nothing but blank space. The LCDs were black, and not a single indicator was lit on the panel.

He pulled the cockpit door closed behind him, uncomfortably aware that the lock didn't snap into place as it clicked shut.

"Tell me this is a prank, Evan. Tell me we haven't really lost power."

The captain shook his head, keeping his attention on the yoke between his legs. "I wish I could. I really, *really* wish I could." He finally turned towards Cole, and the wild panic in his eyes almost knocked the first officer to the ground. "Ben, there was some kind of explosion."

Cole leaned over the back of his seat, reflexively scanning the dead instrument panel for warning lights that might pinpoint the source of the problem. "Where was it? You think the fire suppression system still works?"

The captain shook his head. "No, you don't understand. Not *in here*. I'm saying there was an explosion *out there*. On the horizon. Something big." He stared out the window as if expecting another blast at any moment. "Ben, I think it might have been a nuke."

Cole almost laughed at the absurd suggestion, but Evan's terrified expression had him too spooked to find any humor in the situation. "Are you crazy? If there was a nuke we'd be able to see the mushroom cloud, right? Do you see anything even vaguely mushroom shaped out there? Trust me, if you saw a nuke we'd know about it."

Evan shook his head firmly. "No, not if it was at high altitude. You only get a mushroom cloud from ground level explosions. It's the debris ejected into the atmosphere that causes it, not the bomb itself. If something was set off in the upper atmosphere we'd only see the flash, and that's exactly what I saw: a huge flash on the horizon."

"And you looked directly at it? Come on, if it was a nuke you'd be blind!"

"That only happens at close proximity. Even the biggest nukes can only blind you up to a few dozen miles from the blast. Ben, believe me, I'm not crazy. I saw a hell of a flash on the horizon, and about ten seconds later everything went dead. Engines, electronics, comms, all gone. We're gliding."

"What about the APU?" Cole reached up and toggled a switch marked APU GEN 1 on the panel above his head. Nothing happened.

"No response. It's like the whole system's just *gone*. Completely fried."

Cole felt his heart pound in his chest. The Auxiliary Power Unit was the 737's get out of jail free card, an emergency backup generator in the tail of the plane that could provide enough power for the critical systems to get a stricken plane safely to the ground. The APU was supposed to be untouchable, almost completely isolated from the primary systems so it would be unaffected in the event of a cascading power surge.

"What about the EMDP?" The Electric Motor Driven Pump was designed to keep the hydraulic systems pressurized. It converted the energy of the windmilling engine fans into hydraulic pressure, giving a pilot help with the movement of the control surfaces even when the engines weren't running.

"Nada. Like I said, it's like the whole system's fried. We have *nothing*."

Cole shook his head in disbelief. This shouldn't be possible. The 737 had redundancies built on redundancies several layers deep. Losing one critical system was something passengers would be alarmed to hear happened all the time, but a complete shutdown of *everything* was... hell, it was something that only ever happened in a simulator, and only then at the hands of a sadistic instructor who wanted to torment a trainee with a real life version of the Kobayashi Maru no-win scenario. It wasn't a reality any pilot would expect to face in a dozen lifetimes in the air. For everything to fail all at once, from the engine fuel pumps to the APU to the instrument panel, it'd take nothing short of...

Oh...

Oh no...

"You think it could have been an EMP?"

The captain nodded. There was no surprise in his expression, no look of shock at the suggestion. It was clear he'd already come to the same conclusion.

"I didn't want to be the first to say it, but yeah. It's the only explanation that occurs to me."

Cole's thoughts immediately turned to the people on the ground. What did this mean? Was the US under attack? Had there been some kind of accidental nuclear detonation? Would there even be anything left for them to find once they reached the ground?

He shook his head, waving away the troubling thoughts. Right now it made no difference to them what was going on on the ground. Worrying about it would only be a distraction. All that mattered right now was that he and Evan were piloting a seventy ton glider carrying more than a hundred passengers.

The plane was deadstick. It was going to hit the ground sooner or later, guaranteed. The only question was whether it would be a hard or soft landing, and if anyone would be left alive to walk away afterwards.

Cole took a deep breath and scanned the instrument panels, trying to fight off panic. "OK, let's run through the checklist. What's operational?"

"Nothing but standby instruments. We have altitude, airspeed and heading," Evan replied, tapping the backup mechanical readouts in the center panel. "We have the gravity-fed landing gear, but the control surfaces are all manual reversion." He shot Cole a worried look. "You ever flown manual? I tried it a time or two in the simulator, and to be honest I'm not sure I have the strength."

"Don't worry, I can take over." Cole jerked his chin to the side, directing Evan out of the pilot's seat. At any other time it would be grossly offensive for a first officer to order a more senior pilot out of his chair, but Evan stepped aside gratefully. This was no time for pride. Evan knew that Cole was the best man to have at the yoke for a manual landing.

Without electrical or hydraulic power it was possible to fly a 737 manually, using nothing but the physical strength of the pilot to move the elevators and flaps. In normal flight the plane could be controlled with the lightest touch from the pilot, aided by hydraulic assistance to take the strain, but now... now it would be like driving a car with busted power steering through a pool of molasses. Every little movement of the plane that fought against gravity would be like arm wrestling the sky.

Cole dropped into the pilot's seat and took the yoke in his hands, immediately feeling the firm pull of gravity against the controls. Without power the plane naturally wanted to nose down. The elevators on the tail were being pushed down by the force of the air passing over them, and Cole's biceps strained just to keep the yoke from pushing forward.

"Evan, you gotta find me somewhere to put this thing down. We're overweight and we don't have the power to dump fuel, and if my math is right we have maybe sixty miles of glide left before we reach the ground. There's no way we're making it to Norfolk."

Evan reached into the pocket beside the copilot seat and pulled out a sheaf of charts, spreading them across the dead instrument panel. "OK, let's see... we have Lynchburg, Danville and Emporia Greenville on our flight path, but..." he used his fingers to crudely estimate distance. "You'll come in far too steep for Lynchburg and Danville, unless you think you can put this thing in a 360 glide. And Emporia... shit, we're coming up about fifteen miles short. Do you think you can buy us a little more distance?"

Cole shook his head. "Not a hope. Maybe if I had a

little more altitude to play with, but we've already lost four thousand feet. What about the interstate? We'll cross the 85, right?"

"That's a no go. I know that road, and it's not nearly wide enough for us. Forest on both sides, and lots of flyovers. We'd tear off the wings the second we touched down."

Cole punched his thigh in frustration, glancing nervously at the altimeter. Twenty four thousand feet and falling fast. "OK, just find me some level ground. Farmland. Anything away from the woods or populated areas. Then get back there and warn people we're coming in hard."

He gripped the yoke and pushed forward, nudging the airspeed higher but losing altitude even more rapidly. He'd need to bring the plane in as slow and level as possible if they were to have any hope of surviving the landing, but it was a delicate balancing act. If their airspeed dropped *too* low there was the risk of a wing stall, with too little air flowing over the wings to provide lift. Even now Cole could feel the telltale judder in the airframe that threatened the approach of a stall, and he pushed the yoke forward even further to compensate. If the wing stalled the plane would turn in an instant from a glider to a brick, and without power there was little chance he'd be able to pull it out of a fatal spin.

Evan spread the chart across the center console,

pointing to an area in central Virginia. "OK, here. The Sandy River reservoir. Flat as a pancake for miles around, and it looks to be surrounded by farmland. Set us to zero niner three and descend to…" he quickly performed the mental math, "seven thousand. At this time of day you should see the water from a few miles away."

Cole nodded, twisting the yoke to the right with great difficulty until he hit the correct heading, and then began his descent. "OK, I'm good here. Get back to Samantha and give her the five minute warning."

"You sure you don't need me?"

Cole shook his head. "I need you to get everyone ready. This is all for nothing if we kill the passengers on the way down. Get them braced and then strap yourself in somewhere. Don't be a hero."

Evan climbed out of his seat and gave Cole a pat on the shoulder, about as close to a hug as he'd ever been able to manage. "Good luck," he said, and without another word he left the cockpit, leaving Cole alone to watch the ground quickly approach.

In five minutes this plane would be on the ground. Cole didn't want to admit it, but he was almost certain that neither he nor any of the passengers would still be alive in six.

•▾•

:::4:::

THE SANDY RIVER reservoir was as flat as a millpond, a mud brown, half mile wide pan of settled water, fringed to the east by thick forest and to the west by sprawling fields of tobacco. A hundred yards from the water's edge a small, ramshackle farmhouse sat at the end of an unpaved track, and on the porch outside an elderly woman still wrapped in her nightgown sat in an old steamer chair with a mug of coffee cradled in her hands.

She watched the plane approach curiously at first, flying low over the forest. At this distance – and with her failing eyesight – she thought it might be a Forestry Service plane. Every year or two they sent an old Soviet Antonov fitted out with a scoop to collect water from the reservoir to drop over forest fires in the area. Folks would come from miles around to watch the plane skim the surface of the reservoir like a skipped stone, if only because it was the only mildly interesting thing to ever happen within fifty miles of Sandy River.

As the plane approached, though, it became clear even with her poor eyesight that this was much larger than an Antonov. It passed over the forest silently, a hulking mass crabbing slightly to the right, nose up, and it was only when the enormous landing gear began to deploy that she realized it was a commercial jet. Her coffee mug fell to the ground unnoticed.

The plane came in low and fast, gliding just a few dozen yards above the forest, eerily quiet but for the rush of air across its wings. It looked as if the pilot was struggling to keep the nose up, desperate to clear the trees before touching down, and the woman held her breath as the gear brushed the highest branches. The forest seemed to violently sway in the wake of the plane, the trees pushed from side to side like blades of grass in the turbulence it kicked up.

Just a moment after the tail cleared the edge of the forest the pilot pulled the nose high, and she gasped as the rear wheels hit the ground, bounced twice and then settled on the field, carving a deep furrow through the earth.

She imagined that such a heavy plane would glide to a halt quickly on the soft, loamy soil, but it seemed to continue across the field just as quickly as it would on a paved runway. It looked as if the brakes weren't working, and the flaps on the wings that usually raised to act as air brakes for a landing plane were only now beginning to move into place.

It obviously wouldn't be enough. There was no way the plane would stop before it hit the reservoir, and there seemed to be nothing the pilot could do about it. The woman watched in silent horror as the enormous jet, now moving at something approaching highway speeds, reached the water's edge, lifting for a moment on the raised embankment before slamming down onto the flat surface, sending a huge bow wave rippling out across the muddy water.

She turned and rushed back into her home, cursing her husband for leaving early with the truck, and hunted across the kitchen counter until she found her cell phone. By the time she returned to the porch and dialed 911 the plane was fully immersed, tipping to one side with the right wing jutting from the water like a swimmer waving for help.

The old woman pulled the phone from her ear and cursed with frustration. The call wouldn't go through. In the corner of the screen there were no bars. She frowned. That never happened. There was a cell tower just a mile to the east, so there was always a strong signal at the farm.

The plane was already beginning to sink beneath the surface. The cockpit was almost fully submerged and the raised wing was already beginning to sink, but she couldn't seen anyone climbing out.

She looked down at her phone once again.

Still no bars.

•▼•

:::5:::

THE FOLLOWING MORNING, 3AM
BEYOND WILLOW FALLS

JIM SHEPHERD LAY awkwardly on the roof of the Jeep, his Vanguard Spirit 10x42 binoculars pressed up against his eyes. In the blackness of the town two miles distant the only thing he could clearly see was the roaring fire that engulfed the gas station at the north end of Main Street. Everything else was cast in murky shades of gray and black.

It didn't matter. He was barely paying any attention to the town in any case. For the last hour he'd been staring blindly into the darkness and replaying the shortwave radio broadcast in his mind, over and over, as if with enough repetitions it might start to make some sort of sense.

The President was dead. Somehow, despite all its high tech shielding, Air Force One had been taken down by the EMP. On any other day that would be enough to crowd out any other thought. The nation would come crashing to a halt as the people mourned and, in some cases, quietly celebrated and waited for the earliest moment they thought they could get away with tweeting the tasteless jokes they had ready and waiting. Whatever their opinion of the President might be, though, his death would instantly take the top spot on everyone's list of 'where were you when...' events. JFK, the Moon landing, 9/11, and now this. A President assassinated on American soil by an invading army.

But right now... right now whatever was going on in D.C. felt like it was happening a million miles away, in another country. On another planet. Right now Shepherd was looking down at his home town, and all he could think about was that somewhere in that inky blackness virtually everyone he knew was probably either dead or captured.

Why?

Seriously, *why*? What the hell was the end game here? Shepherd had been turning it over and over in his head, trying to figure out some kind of common sense explanation, but for the life of him he couldn't get a grip on the question. What did the North Koreans think they were doing? What kind of a strategy *was* this? Were they really crazy enough to believe they could conquer three hundred twenty million Americans just by shutting off the power and taking them by surprise? Did they think the people would just roll over and take it? Did they really believe that Americans would give up without a fight, like North Korean peasants beaten down and cowed by decades of fear and oppression? Had they not heard that there were more guns in the US than people, and that millions of those people *lived* for the chance to defend their homeland?

It made no sense at all to Shepherd, but a disturbing image kept pushing itself to the forefront of his mind, a snatched memory from some old BBC nature documentary about hermit crabs. He remembered the narrator describing how, several times over the course of its life, a hermit crab would outgrow its shell, discarding it and hunting for a new and more comfortable home. Most crabs searched until they found a suitable empty shell to move into, but the documentary showed footage of one, a crab that lived in a cracked and disintegrating shell, that tried to move into a shell that was already occupied. It climbed inside, attacking the much larger occupant with its pincers and attempting to tear it out. The attacker was killed, of course, but not before the larger crab lost two legs in the attack.

The narrator described this behavior as inexplicable. He said it was unclear why the crab would attack a much larger enemy simply to find a new shell, but Shepherd thought it seemed perfectly obvious what was happening. The crab was desperate. It knew it couldn't survive in its old, crumbling shell, and even though it knew that the chances of victory against a much larger foe were vanishingly small it was worth the risk, since the alternative was certain death.

Through the binoculars Shepherd could see virtually nothing in the town, but his imagination filled the darkness with a suitable image. Unseen in the blackness below the town crawled, every surface covered in writhing, snapping hermit crabs desperate for one last chance at survival, willing to lash out and attack despite knowing they would almost certainly die.

The only question was how much damage they would inflict before they were beaten.

"You're not gonna see anything over yonder, Shep." Big Joe peered up through his half moon spectacles from the ground below. "Not before daybreak, anyhow. Come on, climb on down and eat something. You'll be no good to anyone starved."

Shepherd shook his head, still staring through the binoculars. "Nah, I'm good. I ate a Snickers a little while ago."

Big Joe let out an exasperated sigh. "You're not a kid any more, Jim. You can't survive on just candy bars. I got some tinned stew going to waste over here. We've already had our fill, and if you don't eat it it's going to the raccoons."

Shep sighed, realizing his gut was rumbling with hunger. "OK, OK. Thanks, Joe. I'll be down in just a few—" He suddenly tensed, pulling the binoculars closer to his eyes. "Hold up, looks like we got company."

"Where? What is it?"

Shepherd squinted into the binoculars, steadying himself on his elbows. "I don't know. Looks like a vehicle leaving town to the north, fast. I think... wait... *crap*. Yeah, it's headed in our direction." He rolled off the roof of the truck in one smooth motion, landing like a cat beside Big Joe. "Time to leave. *Abi!* Come on, we gotta go!"

There was no response.

"Joe, where the hell's Abi?"

"She's taking a... you know... she's gone for a *visit*, Shep. Said she was heading into the trees for some privacy."

"Damn it," Shepherd growled. "We need to get out of here *now*. Whoever's coming, they're gonna pass by here in just a couple of minutes."

He scanned the road and saw there was nowhere they could possibly hide the trucks. On one side of the road was a steep rise climbing into the dense forest, and on the other a steel crash barrier blocked the edge of the hill just a couple of yards from the asphalt. They were penned in. "OK, we gotta hide. You got your gun?"

Big Joe tapped the bulge beneath his jacket. "Always."

"Gimme your keys." He rushed to the hood of the Jeep and lifted it until it latched, then did the same with Joe's truck. An almost useless gesture, he knew, but it couldn't hurt to make the trucks look as if they were broken down and abandoned. "Now, which way did Abi go?" he asked, swinging his Mossberg over his back and tucking the bagged up Ruger in the crook of his arm.

Big Joe shrugged and pointed vaguely into the woods to the side of the road, on the other side of the crash barrier. "I didn't think it proper to look, but I think she went down that way."

"Then let's go, and pray she doesn't like to whistle while she pees."

Big Joe dropped to his knees and crawled beneath the barrier as Shepherd vaulted it, and as they vanished into the trees Shepherd called out Abi's name, much more quietly now. He could already hear the throaty grumbling of the approaching engine, though it was hard to tell if it was close or if it only *sounded* close in the silence of the night.

"*Abi!*" he hissed. "Damn it, how much privacy does a woman need to go to the bathroom?"

Big Joe let out a humorless chuckle and shook his head. "I stopped asking questions like that long ago, Shep. Not the kind of thing you'll ever hear answered in a way that makes a lick of sense."

"OK, keep an eye on the woods. If you see her,

stop her. I'm gonna go watch the road for… wait a sec. You said you were cooking up a stew. Where is it?"

"Behind the truck, out of the breeze." It seemed to take Joe a moment to figure out the problem. "Oh hell, I left the gas burner on."

"Damn it, Joe!"

"I'm sorry, I wasn't exactly expecting company, you know? I didn't think we'd have to run at a moment's notice."

Shepherd passed the gun bag down to Joe and held out his hand. "Give me your Sig, then go find Abi and hide. I'll yell when it's safe to come out."

Big Joe held a protective hand against the holster beneath his jacket. "You want my gun?"

Shepherd nodded. "Abi has my Glock, and I've only got three shells left in the Mossberg before reloading. If these people aren't friendly I don't want to be standing up there with just my dick in my hand, know what I'm saying?"

Big Joe scowled as he lifted the catch on the holster and pulled out his modified Sig Sauer P238. "You just better come back with that gun or not at all, Jim Shepherd. That's the only pistol I can fire with these." He held up his short, stubby fingers. "I don't want to be left with *my* dick in my hand, either. Not unless you want those Koreans to die laughing."

Shepherd took the gun and tucked it beneath his belt. "Don't worry, I don't intend to do any shooting. I just want a little insurance in case anyone gets too curious." He turned back towards the road and listened for the approaching engine. "OK, scram. Find Abi, and get her somewhere safe."

Joe reluctantly turned and walked deeper into the woods, whispering Abi's name as he went, and Shepherd began the climb through the undergrowth back towards the trucks. The vehicle was definitely close now, the sound of its throaty engine carried on the light breeze. He stopped and cocked his head. It was something big, like the truck he'd found on the road into Monroeville the previous day.

He finally reached the edge of the forest just a few yards back from the crash barrier, dropping to the ground and pulling the Mossberg from his shoulder. As the engine grew louder he looked over the Sig Sauer to make damned sure it was ready to fire if the situation required it.

Shepherd had never used Big Joe's gun before, and he was surprised at just how small and light it felt. He'd only ever seen it holstered, and against Joe's diminutive frame it had seemed like a good sized gun that could pack a decent punch, but in his hands it felt like a toy compared to the Glock.

As the headlights of the approaching vehicle began to play on the leaves of the trees above him he started to worry that maybe he didn't have enough firepower. Three shells in the Mossberg and a six round magazine for the little pocket pistol would never be enough if it came down to a firefight against—

Oh, no.

Shepherd felt the blood in his veins turn to battery acid as he saw the figure emerging from the woods on the other side of the road. Joe had been wrong. Abi hadn't gone down the hill to find some privacy, but *up*. She must have been surprised to hear the sound of an engine, because she was running down the hill as if she was afraid she'd be left behind. She must have thought the rumbling engine was Shep or Joe's truck, getting ready to leave.

It was already too late to yell out a warning. Abi emerged from the tree line at a fast jog trailing a roll of toilet paper from her hand, and the headlights of the approaching vehicle caught her full on. She froze, suddenly realizing what was going on, then she turned on her heels, quickly darted back into the forest and vanished behind the dense bushes.

The engine tone was already changing. The approaching vehicle slowed and pulled to a halt just as it came into view in the gap between the ground and the steel crash barrier, and Shepherd's heart sank. It was military, a beat up old troop truck decked out in green camo paint, just like the one they'd seen on his street as the soldiers moved from house to house. He gripped the Sig tighter, expecting at any moment to see armed Koreans come pouring out from beneath the canvas awning that shrouded the rear.

Shepherd held his breath as the truck sat in the middle of the road, and as the engine died he quietly pulled back the hammer of the Sig. Maybe he'd be able to take them by surprise. Maybe he'd be able to empty the magazine as the troops emerged, then unload the Mossberg into the driver's window before he started to run. He knew he'd never be able to take out an entire truck full of soldiers, but at least he could distract them and give Abi a running start.

He slowly pulled himself up to a crouch, using the cover of the crash barrier to creep towards the truck, but as he moved closer the sound of muffled voices emerged from the back.

English speaking voices.

"Keep pressure on the wound!"

"Damn it, I can't find the artery. There's too much blood!"

"Come on, man, stay with us. Just keep your eyes on me, OK? Right here, on me. Come on, buddy, stay awake."

The panicked voices eventually subsided, replaced only by a weak, wet gasping sound, like the gurgle of water running down a drain. Finally even that faded, and all Shepherd could hear was a gentle weeping from beneath the awning.

"Don't blame yourself. There was nothing you

could have done," came a man's voice. "Once that femoral artery gets severed it's only a matter of time."

Shepherd stood from behind the crash barrier, gently decocking the hammer of the Sig. "Hello?"

The weeping stopped. Beneath the awning the silence took on a different, more guarded tone. Shepherd could almost feel the tension of the occupants, even though he couldn't see them.

"It's OK, I'm American. I'm friendly." He tucked the Sig beneath his belt and slung the Mossberg over his shoulder. "Ummm... is it safe for me to approach the truck?"

The silence continued for a beat, and then another. Shepherd was well aware that anyone inside the vehicle could easily fire out through the canvas, and almost subconsciously he crouched a little to regain what little cover was offered by the crash barrier.

At the back of the vehicle the canvas flap was pushed aside with a rustle that sounded deafening in the silence, and Shepherd heard feet hit the ground. He gripped the shoulder strap of Mossberg a little tighter, ready to swing it around at a moment's notice, but he tried to stand as casually as possible. The last thing he wanted was a gunfight with fellow Americans.

"It's OK, you can come out," he called to the invisible figure standing at the back of the truck. "I'm not a threat. I'm from Willow Falls, the town down the hill."

He flinched a little as the figure finally emerged, and then relaxed when he saw that the man wasn't obviously armed. He stood around six feet tall, his dark hair cut short, and he looked like he'd spent the day swimming through a swamp. His hands and the front of his shirt were covered in fresh blood, but beneath it all were the torn remains of a pilot's uniform.

"Hang on." The man held up a hand. "Just…" He took a deep breath, his face turning white. "Just hang on a sec." A moment later he doubled over by the rear wheel of the truck, and Shepherd turned away and cringed at the sound of retching. He tried to ignore the splash of vomit on the asphalt, and he was relieved when the man finally spat and stood up straight, his eyes bloodshot.

"Sorry, I just… we…" He waved towards the back of the truck. "Doesn't matter," the man said, nodding to Shepherd's shoulder as he wiped his mouth with the back of his hand. "Would you mind setting down the shotgun? Makes me a little nervous."

Shepherd hesitated for a moment, then he nodded, placing the shotgun carefully on the ground, and as a gesture of goodwill he slowly pulled the Sig from his belt, showed it to the pilot and set it down alongside the Mossberg.

"Thanks. What's your name?" the pilot asked.

"Jim. Jim Shepherd. Like I said I'm from the town down the hill. You just came from there, right? What's going on?"

The pilot nodded. "Yeah, we... we just escaped from there." He looked down at his hands. "It's bad down there. Bad everywhere."

"How'd you get out? What's happening down there? Are they killing people?"

The pilot started to answer, but he fell silent as the canvas awning at the back of the truck was pushed aside. A young woman climbed down, and he rushed to her side as someone in the truck began to lower a body slowly out the back. It was another man, also dressed in a pilot's uniform. The bottom half of his shirt was covered in blood, and his trousers had been torn open to access a wound somewhere beneath.

The pilot gently lowered the body to the ground, cushioning the back of the man's head with his hand. Shepherd rushed over, shrugged off his denim jacket and placed it respectfully over his face. The young woman wept, unwilling to let go of the man's hand.

The pilot closed his eyes and whispered a quiet prayer over the body as Shepherd stood back. For a long moment the road was silent but for the whispers and the weeping, and Shepherd barely noticed as Abi and Big Joe appeared cautiously at the front of the truck.

"Everything OK here, Shep?" asked Joe, as Abi rushed to the side of the young woman. Joe looked nervous and guarded, unsure of what was happening. "You guys need any help with anything?"

The pilot looked up at Big Joe, wiping a tear from his cheek. He saw the gun bag slung over Joe's shoulder, the barrel of the Ruger poking out from the open zipper.

"Just one thing," he said, looking back at the body on the asphalt, his fists clenched white with anger. "Do you guys have more guns?"

•▼•

:::**6**:::

THE MORNING OF JULY 4TH
SANDY RIVER RESERVOIR

BEN COLE OPENED his eyes to a familiar sight, suddenly made alien.

The cockpit was bathed in a deep, shimmering green glow, as if it was trapped at the bottom of an aquarium. As Cole groggily raised his head from the yoke he'd slammed into as the plane ground to a halt a torrent of muddy water caught him full in the face, blinding him and stealing the air from his lungs. One of the windows had shattered on impact, and the cockpit was quickly filling as the plane sank beneath the surface.

He jerked in his seat to escape the torrent, reached beneath the surface and blindly fumbled at the seat belt tight around his waist. When he finally released the clasp and escaped from the seat the cold, churning water was already up to his chest and quickly rising. Freed from the belt the force of the torrent swept him from his seat, pushing him back towards the cockpit door, and he reached out and grasped the handle firmly, holding himself in place. He tugged it down, braced his legs clumsily against the jump seat at the rear of the cockpit and pushed.

Nothing happened. The door didn't budge.

What the hell? Was it locked? Had it buckled in the crash? He felt his panic rise as the water reached his neck. The last of the daylight vanished from the top of the windows as the cockpit sank deeper into the water, and he was plunged into near darkness as he pushed at the door again. This time he managed to push it open an inch or two before he lost his grip, and it slammed closed.

"Shit," he cursed, taking in a mouth full of brackish water. There must be water on the other side of the door, forcing it closed until the pressure equalized.

Cole felt a sudden surge of panic as a terrifying memory bubbled to the surface of his mind. He'd been in this situation once before, years earlier, in a mocked up cockpit at the bottom of a pool as part of his flight training. To pass the ditching course he'd had to escape a submerged cockpit, make it to the emergency exit and reach a life raft floating on the surface. That had been terrifying enough, but back in training he'd been decked out in a wet suit with an emergency rebreather and safety personnel just out of sight, and he'd had lights to guide the way. He knew he hadn't been in any real danger, but even then the claustrophobic panic had almost overwhelmed him.

Now he was alone and in the dark, trapped in a cockpit quickly filling with cold and murky water. This was *nothing* like the training. There was no rebreather waiting to fill his lungs with life-giving oxygen, and there were no divers waiting on the other side of the door to rescue him. There was only rising water, and darkness, and panic.

He scanned his eyes around the cockpit before turning back to the windows, desperate for another way out, but even in the near darkness he could see he'd never be able to squeeze his way through a frame that small. The door was the only possible escape route.

The churning, frothing water was almost at the ceiling now. He couldn't touch the floor. Couldn't even *see* the floor through the murk. He swam up to the surface, taking a stale, gasping breath as he reached the shrinking air pocket, and he grabbed hold of the edge of a ceiling panel to hold himself steady.

There were only a few seconds of air left. He had to lift his chin just to keep his mouth above the surface, and he knew that as soon as the air pocket shrank to nothing he'd only have one chance to escape. He'd have one more breath, and if he didn't make it out the door it would be the last he'd ever take.

Cole's survival instincts kicked in without conscious thought. He took a final deep breath, plunged beneath the water and kicked his feet up to the surface, using them to brace against the ceiling as he reached out for the door handle. His searching fingers missed at the first attempt, and then once more, but on the third he took a firm grip and twisted it down.

The door cracked open an inch, and on the other side a dim shaft of daylight played through the water. Feeling his resolve stiffen he braced his legs firmly against the ceiling, pressed both hands against the door and pushed with all his strength.

It opened.

He felt his lungs burning now. The effort of pushing the door had drained his reserves, and he could feel the pain in his lungs as his oxygen-starved brain begged him to take a deep breath. The urge to open his mouth and breathe in was almost irresistible, even though he knew there'd be no oxygen waiting for him. He forced the urge from his mind, kicking forward into the cabin as his heavy clothing tried to drag him back. Nothing but pain now. Burning, overwhelming pain, as if his lungs were on fire.

He forced himself to pause despite the agony, opening his eyes and scanning the cabin. Up ahead towards the back of the plane he saw a flash of yellow, but as he watched the cabin was plunged into blackness as the rear of the plane sank beneath the surface.

He turned to his right, and he almost lost control when he saw the emergency door was wide open. The plane was tilted down towards the door, and escaping would mean swimming down before he could swim up. The thought of descending deeper into the water was horrifying, but it didn't matter. It was *out*. A moment closer to a blissful breath.

He kicked against the drinks cart drifting against the side wall of the flight attendant's area, forcing his body forward and down, out of the cabin and into the open water. As soon as he was out he could feel the sucking sensation of the enormous plane as it plunged towards the lake bed. It was trying to drag him down with it, as if unwilling to go down without its pilot, but Cole wasn't ready to acquiesce. He braced his feet against the top of the open door and kicked with all his strength, his arms reaching out ahead of him with hands outstretched, as if to drag the daylight closer.

The surface seemed impossibly distant. There was barely any light down this deep, and what little reached down so far looked like it was coming from a mile above, as if at the end of an impossibly long tunnel. Cole kicked towards it, clumsily thrashing his legs to propel himself forward and upward, but with a sinking feeling he realized he'd never make it back to the surface before his lungs gave out, no matter how hard he kicked. It was just too far, and he had nothing left to give.

He could already feel his resolve slipping. He knew that any moment now the temptation to take a breath would grow stronger than his resolve to keep his lips sealed. It was already gripping him. Just seconds now. He kicked weakly, but even with all his strength it felt like he was moving no closer towards the surface. If anything he felt as if he was sinking deeper, dragged down to rejoin the plane as it settled in the soft, silty blackness of the lake bed.

Colored spots flashed before his eyes as his vision began to shrink down to a tunnel. He didn't dare look away from the light far above, but he knew without looking that his legs were no longer kicking. Every ounce of his remaining energy was given over to keeping his lips pressed shut, and it was all he could do to weakly row his arms.

The light above began to blink out as his consciousness drifted away. His tightly closed lips began to pry open, and he knew that a breath was on the way. He wanted to scream, but there was nothing there. No air. No strength. No hope.

All he could do was open his mouth.

Bubbles of stale air escaped from his lips and flitted past his eyes on their way to the distant surface above, quickly replaced by muddy water that seared his throat and lungs as it forced its way into his body.

The painful fire of a moment ago was nothing compared to this. It felt as if a flamethrower had been shoved down his throat and ignited. The pain was like nothing he'd ever experienced, an agonizing, searing knife thrust into every nerve ending. He opened his mouth in a silent, airless scream, but all it brought was more pain.

Unconsciousness finally began to close in through the agony, and Cole welcomed it... embraced it. The only emotion he could feel, in that tiny, sane corner of his mind that wasn't gripped by panic and terror, was relief. Relief that at least this pain would soon be over. At least it was just a passing sensation, soon to be replaced by blissful nothingness.

His body began to thrash and convulse as the darkness closed in. The patch of light above him shrank to a circle, and then a dot, and then nothing at all. The pain was already fading, a distant memory experienced by someone else.

As the blackness took him his life flickered out like a spent votive, its prayer unheard and unanswered.

...

....

.....

For a few moments and a boundless eternity there was nothing.

.....

....

...

... Pain...

... Crushing...

... Searing...

The fire climbed from Cole's lungs and rushed to his throat, followed by a terrifying, agonizing suffocation. He tried to take a breath but only caught more water. Acrid vomit climbed from his stomach and met the brackish water in his throat, and the sharp, acid brew coughed itself into the air, running down his chin and pooling in the hollow of his neck.

"Breathe, Ben, *breathe!*"

He finally managed to take a wet, sucking breath, half air and half vomit, and almost immediately he puked again, this time managing to turn his head.

"Come on, take a breath! You can do it!"

With a superhuman effort Cole managed to suck in oxygen, forcing himself to endure the burning in his throat until the air finally reached his lungs. Once the first ragged breath came more followed, greedily gulped until he collapsed into a coughing fit that sent his ears ringing and threatened to steal away his consciousness once more.

Eventually his breath returned, and once it came through more smoothly he opened his bloodshot eyes, immediately squeezing them closed when they filled with stinging mud.

"Hold up there, buddy, just stay calm. Sam, go wet something down to clean him up."

For a moment he lay still, his burning eyes squeezed tight, until he felt something cool and wet run across his face. He fought against it, afraid it would stop him breathing again, and he tried to sit up as he opened his eyes once again.

The blurred image slowly resolved. Evan and Samantha looming over him, their blurred expressions concerned. He was... where was he? Cool grass beneath him. The sun was hot, and already his wet, muddy clothes had begun to cling to his skin as they dried. He choked down the urge to vomit and forced himself up on his elbows.

"How many fingers, Ben?" Evan held up a hand, and Cole tried to focus. "Come on, how many fingers."

"Three?" Evan frowned, and as Cole tried to repeat the answer he realized his voice was slow and slurred. "Three." He coughed, spitting out a mouthful of gritty water and acid vomit, and forced the words out slowly, deliberately, trying to regain control of his numb lips and his foggy mind. "Three... fingers."

"Attaboy." Evan gripped him by his shoulder. "Thought we'd lost you for a minute there."

Cole rolled to his side and dug his fingers into the soil. "What happened? How did I..." His voice was hoarse, little more than a strained whisper.

"Just rest, OK? Take it easy for a minute. I have to go help the others."

"Others?" Cole looked around. Maybe three dozen passengers lay on the grass, most of them frozen in a state of shock, some weeping. An elderly man to his right looked dead, his papery skin pale and his chest still. A woman above him was desperately trying to resuscitate him, but it didn't appear to be working.

"What happened?" he asked Samantha, pulling himself up to a sitting position. "Is this all that made it?"

The flight attendant nodded tearfully. "Oh, Ben, it was *awful*. They wouldn't listen to us. We tried to tell them but they just wouldn't listen!"

"Tell them what?" It still hurt to speak. Every word felt like razor blades in his throat.

Samantha wiped a tear away. "The life jackets. They wouldn't listen, and once a couple of them did it they all joined in."

"Sam, slow down. What are you talking about?"

Samantha took a deep breath, visibly gathering herself. "There were a couple of passengers in first class. Young idio— no, I shouldn't say that. Young guys. As soon as we hit the water they grabbed their life jackets and inflated them. I told them not to, but they wouldn't listen to me." She looked around at the small group of survivors. "Then almost everyone did the same as soon as they saw them. We tried yelling, but…" She shook her head. "As soon as we got the door open the water came rushing in. There was nothing we could do. Everyone just got swept up to the back of the plane, you know, like corks in water. We couldn't get up there to help them."

A terrible memory surfaced in Cole's mind. He'd *seen* them. He'd seen the patch of yellow up at the back of the cabin as he'd escaped, and as it sank in he felt guilt stab at his heart as he realized he was thankful he didn't know they were people at the time. He was glad he hadn't needed to make the call: escape or help. He knew he never would have lived if he'd tried to help.

He could barely imagine the hell the trapped passengers must have gone through, even after he'd been through it himself. There had been a hundred twenty passengers on the flight, and no more than forty were out here on the grass. That meant eighty men, women and children had been swept all the way to the back of the cabin, crushed together as their air pocket shrank to nothing above them. Maybe they hadn't been able to reach the rear door in the crush. Maybe they couldn't see it. Maybe they didn't know how it opened. Their only way of escaping would have been to shrug off their life vests and swim thirty yards down in the darkness to the front door, but with eighty passengers pressed together in the narrow cabin, each of them fighting to reach the shrinking air pocket at the back of the plane...

What a hell of a way to die.

"Jesus," he whispered, even more thankful now that he'd been able to open the cockpit door. If the plane had gone down tail first he could have found his own escape blocked. "Are you OK?" he asked. "Are you injured?"

Samantha shook her head. "No, I'm fine, but some of us weren't so lucky." She nodded at the small crowd. "We have two broken legs, maybe four people with cracked ribs and a couple with a concussion. We need to get these people to a hospital, but the captain says he can't reach anyone. None of the phones that survived the water are getting any signal. There's an old lady at a house over there who says her husband should be home soon with his truck, but the captain says he doesn't think the guy's coming back."

Samantha leaned in and lowered her voice conspiratorially. "He won't tell me what's going on, but I know something's wrong. Ben, what's happening here?"

•▼•

:::7:::

FOUR HOURS DRAGGED by before reality finally began to set in among the survivors.

Cole and the captain had corralled the bruised and battered group into the farmhouse, thanking the old lady who lived there for letting them mess up her clean home with their muddy clothes as they fixed up the injured, and when everyone was finally settled Cole watched as Evan did his best to explain what they thought had happened. He told them about the bright flash in the sky, and the dead electronics. He tried to explain the EMP in simple layman's terms, but he got nothing in return but chuckles and disbelieving stares.

It was just too shocking a truth to lay on people who'd just come through a plane crash. To go from such a personal trauma to the idea that this was happening to everyone was just too big a leap for most to make. They couldn't wrap their head around the idea that the most terrifying thing they'd ever experienced had also happened to every last passenger in the sky, hundreds of thousands of people plummeting to the ground all in the same moment.

A few of the survivors seemed receptive to the idea. Cole could see in their eyes that they trusted the captain, but the mood of the crowd kept them from speaking up.

That was the trouble with crowds. After years of ferrying hundreds of passengers across the sky every day Cole knew that the average IQ of a group drops ten points every time the group doubles in size, and individual agency vanishes without a trace once you gather ten or more people together in a room. Nobody ever wants to be the guy who rocks the boat. Nobody wants to stand out from the crowd, to have to argue a painful truth against the majority.

And so nobody believed it. Everyone chose instead to reassure one another that this wasn't really happening. That the danger was over. That in five minutes the ambulances and fire trucks would finally appear to whisk them off to safety. No, five minutes from *now*. OK, maybe ten minutes. *Whatever. They're on the way, you'll see. Everything will be fine.*

Hell, Cole could understand why they didn't want to accept the truth. He didn't want to believe it himself, because more likely than not the truth meant that they were all dead men walking.

There was a woman among the survivors, the wife of a man in the group, who'd suffered a nasty compound fracture of the tibia in the crash. Samantha and the captain had done what little they could to stabilize her and clean the wound, but it was still filthy. A spur of dirty gray bone was jutting through the skin, and they had no way to set it straight. The wound was packed with mud, and the woman had screamed in agony when Evan tried to clean it. She needed to get to a hospital right away to have the wound properly irrigated or infection would quickly set in, and if she didn't get the leg set soon it would never heal properly, if she even survived.

Why would her husband want to accept that help wasn't coming? Not only that, but why would he want to accept there wasn't help to be found *anywhere*? That even if they got to a hospital they'd find it in chaos and without power. Cole and Evan were essentially trying to convince this man that his wife was beyond help. Of *course* he didn't want to accept that reality, and of course nobody wanted to tear his hope away from him, not when the lie was so much more comfortable than the truth.

It was only as the hours dragged by that the passengers began to doubt their initial certainty. At first it was just a few concerned looks, a few passing glances between the survivors. *The ambulances should be here by now, right? Why hasn't help arrived?* They still tried to convince each other that there wasn't long to wait, as if their own nerves could be settled if only everyone else believed hard enough, but as time went on the truth began to set in.

By the time two in the afternoon rolled around people were finally ready to speak up. They couldn't deny it any longer. No matter how remote this farmhouse may be there was just no way that a 737 could crash in the middle of Virginia without anyone noticing. There was no way help could be four hours away, when the state capital itself was only seventy miles to the east. This wasn't Alaska. They weren't in the wilderness. Hundreds of people must have seen the plane fall to the ground. Thousands, maybe. There was no earthly explanation for why they were still waiting for help after four hours.

When it seemed as if the majority had finally begun to accept the truth Cole was ready to put his plan in action. Rose, the old lady who owned the house, had an old trailer out back. It wasn't much, just a two wheeled aluminum flat bed with the towing eye hooked up to a rusty old bicycle, but Cole figured it would be large enough to carry the injured.

Rose kindly volunteered to loan the trailer to Cole on the condition that he left it in the parking lot beside the gas station in Rice, a small village three miles to the east, where her husband could pick it up "when he finally gets home, the lazy swine." Rice had a pharmacy, she told him, and a diner where they could eat and wait for help to arrive.

Cole had tried to explain to her about the EMP, to convince her to come with them into town, but the significance of it seemed to sail straight over her head. She couldn't seem to grasp the importance of the power grid being permanently knocked out. It was as if she thought it would be nothing but a temporary inconvenience. "I only watch the TV for the weather report, dear," she assured him. "Can't say I'll miss it if it doesn't work for a while."

It took another hour to load the injured onto the trailer. The woman with the compound fracture screamed in agony when they tried to move her, and it was only when she finally passed out from the pain that they could lift her up, her foot supported as comfortably as possible on a pile of still wet jackets and sweaters gathered from the survivors.

Cole pushed the bike for the first mile, cursing every inch of the poorly paved road. One of the tires of the trailer was flat as a pancake, and in the heat of the early afternoon it was hard going just to keep up a reasonable walking pace. By the time Evan insisted on taking over after forty minutes Cole's shirt was drenched with sweat and clinging to his skin. He gratefully handed over the bike and dropped back, taking a break in the shade of a tree while the group went on ahead.

For five minutes he rested, catching his breath and allowing the soft breeze to dry off his shirt, but nothing did much good. After the strains of the day his energy was gone. He just wanted to be home with a steak and scotch, and the thought that there might be a long road ahead sapped away what little strength he had left. His apartment in Norfolk was almost two hundred miles to the south east. In the hours they'd been on the ground they hadn't seen a single working vehicle, and if that meant *nothing* worked it could be days before he got home to his bed. Weeks, even, and there was no telling if home would even be safe when he got there.

Would there be food? Would the army step in? The National Guard? FEMA? The Red Cross? He didn't have the first clue if there was any kind of plan to deal with a disaster on this scale. Had the folks up at the top ever seriously considered the possibility of an EMP? Did they have a strategy waiting to be rolled out, or was this one of those disasters that caught everyone completely by surprise, and left them fumbling blindly for an answer even as people starved?

"Oh, kill me now," he sighed, pulling himself painfully to his feet and setting off in pursuit of the group. He just prayed there'd be something to eat in Rice. Maybe even a bar where he could grab a drink to relax his aching muscles. Maybe it was too much to hope for, but he—

He stopped in his tracks. There was a sound

coming from the road up ahead.

Cole felt his heart beat a little faster in his chest. He barely wanted to believe it was real, but as it grew louder he realized it wasn't just an illusion. It was the sound of an approaching engine.

Thank you, Jesus! He wanted to laugh out loud in celebration. There was no sweeter sound on earth than that of a vehicle coming to take them to safety. An engine meant there was power. Power meant refrigeration. Air conditioning. A hot shower and a clean set of clothes. A medium rare steak, and an ice cube for his tumbler of scotch. If nothing else it at least meant he wouldn't have to keep walking down this damned road in the interminable heat.

Almost without noticing he broke into a jog, and then a flat out run, suddenly full of energy now he knew he wouldn't have to conserve what little he had left. He was maybe a hundred yards behind the group, and he wanted to be there when the vehicle arrived. He knew he was being selfish, but he wanted to be in the first group if there wasn't enough room to take everyone into town.

Cole's heart soared as the vehicle came into view. It was an Army truck, a beautiful olive green beast of a thing with a canvas awning stretched over the back. It'd be a squeeze, but he was sure they'd be able to fit a few dozen people in the back for the short ride into town, or to wherever they planned to go. Right now

Cole didn't care. Anywhere with food, running water and a soft bed would be fine with him.

The truck slowed just a little ahead of the survivors, and Cole caught up with the back of the group as Samantha began to jump excitedly up and down, smiling from ear to ear. Her enthusiasm was infectious, and by the time the truck pulled to a halt the group was cheering and hollering, a few of the men pumping their fists in the air as the passenger door swung open and a soldier climbed down.

"God bless you!"

"Here comes the cavalry!"

"U.S.A! U.S.A!"

The ruckus and laughter died down a little as a soldier stepped out of the truck, vanishing quickly towards the back. He called out a sharp order, and a few members of the group exchanged concerned glances.

"I didn't get that. Was that English? What did he say?" one woman asked, drawing her daughter just a little closer.

Another man frowned. "Didn't sound English to me. Can anyone get a look at the driver?"

From where the group was standing the flat front window of the truck caught the sun perfectly, obscuring their view of the cab. Cole was about to step towards the truck when he heard movement from the back, and a moment later it all went to hell.

The soldiers appeared from both sides of the truck. A dozen of them, six to a side in a flanking formation, all of them leveling rifles at the group. Cole was taken aback, too shocked to move. Every last one of the soldiers was Asian. His first thought – more hopeful than logical – was that this was just a coincidence. In the few seconds it took them to descend on the group he tried to tell himself it was nothing to worry about, but even as the thought occurred to him he knew it was bullshit.

These soldiers weren't friendly. They weren't here to help.

His fears were confirmed when one yelled an order at another. He didn't pick up on the language but there was no question it wasn't English. The six on the left shouldered their weapons and started yelling at the group, urging them away from the trailer and towards the side of the road. The other six spread out to the right, herding the group like a flock of sheep towards the back of the truck.

"Now hold on a damned second! What the hell do you guys think you're—"

Cole didn't see the man who spoke, but he heard the sickening crunch of bone as the butt of a rifle was thrust into his face. The people around him yelled out with alarm, catching the falling body and helping him to his feet.

"Quiet!" one of the soldiered yelled, taking a step

forward. "Back!" He jerked the barrel of his rifle towards the truck. *"Back! Back!"*

A woman timidly stepped forward, her head dipped fearfully and her eyes cast towards the ground. "Sir, we don't know what you mean. Do you mean stand back, or get in the back of the truck?"

The soldier who gave the order looked confused. It was clear to Cole that he didn't speak more than a few words of English, and he seemed to be weighing up his options, trying to figure out if the woman had been talking back to him. Should he punish her or leave her be?

After a moment's thought he pushed the barrel of his rifle hard against her chest, leaned in and hissed. *"Back!"* With another jerk of the rifle towards the back of the truck she stumbled in that direction, tears streaming down her face, and the rest of the group obediently followed.

Cole felt as if he was locked in a nightmare. None of this felt real, and despite the very real pain in every muscle he couldn't convince himself this wasn't just an extremely vivid dream. The belief was almost enough to spur him to fight back, to play the hero and take on the soldiers hand to hand, but self preservation stopped him from taking a step. This felt just a little too real for him to risk it not being a nightmare.

The soldiers on the left stood over by the trailer of

wounded, looking them over. One stepped forward and touched the leg of the woman with the compound fracture, eliciting an agonized scream. He stepped back, alarmed, and called out a question to the man who'd ordered the group back. He seemed to be the leader, even though none of them seemed to wear any sort of rank or insignia on what looked like old Army surplus uniforms. The leader called back, and in response the first soldier stepped forward and once again poked at the woman's leg, as if to intentionally make her scream.

The leader watched her for a moment, then shook his head. "*Moduluel jug-ida,*" he said, gesturing towards the wounded on the trailer.

They opened fire without another word. There were eight people on the trailer, two with broken legs, four with cracked ribs and two with just a concussion, but the soldiers executed every one of them without a moment's thought. They shot them with as little emotion as a slaughterhouse knocker stuns a cow with a bolt gun.

The husband of the woman with the fracture let out a terrifying primal scream. For a moment Cole wasn't even sure it had come from him, a slightly tubby balding man in his late forties. He didn't look like the kind of person capable of such a rage-filled yell, but then he pushed his way through the group and charged at the soldiers with all the purpose of a linebacker rushing a quarterback.

It took more than one shot to bring him down. There was no hope he'd ever cover the distance and survive, but it seemed as if the soldiers were alarmed that he made it so far before falling. Even after he fell to his knees with four shots in his gut and chest he was still trying to pick himself up. It wasn't until someone managed a head shot that he finally tumbled face first to the ground, a halo of blood spreading on the asphalt around his head.

In the confusion people began to break away from the back of the group, fleeing into the field by the side of the road, but they didn't get far. As soon as the soldiers noticed the movement they opened fire without even calling out a warning or waiting for an order. Cole dropped to the ground and rolled beneath the truck, dragging Samantha along with him. A young woman who'd been standing just beside Cole slumped to her knees and then fell to the side, a rosette of blood blossoming across her chest. She hadn't even been trying to flee. She'd only been standing there, but the man who pulled the trigger didn't give a damn.

Cole lay beneath the truck with his face pressed against the searing asphalt, holding Samantha by the arm so tight she squealed with pain. He loosened his grip, waiting for the gunfire to end before slowly reaching his arms out the side and calling out. "We surrender! Don't shoot!"

The leader walked to the side of the truck and tried to drag him out, a futile effort considering the fact that Cole was six feet tall and two hundred pounds while the soldier looked to be around five seven and a buck fifty soaking wet, but Cole played along. He allowed himself to be pulled out, and when he took to his feet he slouched a little so as not to loom over the guy.

"Back!" the soldier ordered, pointing to the back of the truck.

Cole helped Samantha to her feet and nodded at Evan, hidden from the gunfire behind the truck. "Let's live to fight another day, OK? No dumb moves."

Evan and Samantha both nodded, following him to the back of the truck and climbing in under the canvas. They sat along the wooden benches running down the sides, and by the time the engine fired up there were around ten survivors squeezed in, with the soldiers crouched at the back, weapons ready.

Ten people. Just a few minutes ago there had been forty.

•▼•

:::**8**:::

COLE LOST TRACK of time. For what felt like
hours the truck bounced along the rough back roads
of Virginia, stopping at random intervals. Most of the
time it only stopped for a few minutes. Cole could
hear the front doors open and close, but the soldiers
in the back stayed behind to guard the survivors.
Every so often he'd hear the sound of gunfire,
sometimes close, sometimes distant, and each time
everyone in the group would duck to the floor and
pray that no shots would pierce the canvas awning.
There was no telling what was going on out there. No
more prisoners were brought to join them, and the
soldiers guarding the back of the truck seemed
entirely unfazed by the action outside.

The only time the soldiers got excited was around
sunset. The truck took a hard left off the road,
sending everyone tumbling to the ground, and soon
after it pulled to a sharp stop and the soldiers in the
back jumped down to the ground. Through the gap in
the awning Cole could see some kind of parking lot.
The gap was too tight to see much, but off in the
distance around a hundred yards away he thought he

could see some kind of store.

"These guys are Korean," he whispered, just loud enough for the group to hear.

"How'd you know that?" a young woman asked, her voice shaky after hours of crying.

"I've flown into Incheon a few times." He noticed the blank looks. "It's the airport in Seoul, South Korea. I can't speak a word of the language but I can recognize it, and there's no question. They were speaking Korean."

The woman frowned. "Aren't South Koreans the... you know, the good guys? Aren't they on our side?"

Cole nodded. "Yeah, they are, but they use the same language as the North. It used to be one big country up until the end of World War Two, then the Soviets occupied the North and we occupied the South. These guys have to be North Korean."

Evan waved his hand dismissively. "It doesn't matter who they are right now. All that matters is they're bad guys with guns. Do you think we should try to run?"

Cole looked around at the group. They'd been left completely unguarded, and out the back it seemed like they had a clear run. "I say we go for it. I'd rather die out there than—"

He fell silent when he heard what was going on outside. The soldiers were yelling out orders, and in response came angry voices. American voices.

"Who the hell do you think you are?"

"Hey, these guys ain't real Army!"

"Howie, *shoot 'em!*"

Cole tucked himself into a ball and buried his chin in his chest as gunfire erupted what seemed like just a few yards away. The noise was so loud that it seemed to shake the truck itself, and then it abruptly stopped. In the near silence that followed Cole could only hear the ringing in his ears and the sucking sounds of a final breath being drawn on the floor outside, followed by footsteps fading into the distance.

Samantha was the first to raise her head. "Do you think they're dead?"

Cole nodded. "I don't think our boys won that fight." He raised his voice a little. "Hello? Anyone alive out there?"

The silence dragged on. There was no way of telling if the Americans outside had run or were dead, but Cole knew that to step out beyond the awning would be to invite death. These people didn't screw around, and from what little he could see of the vast expanse of the parking lot outside there didn't seem to be any cover to run to. Running out now would be like trying to cross no man's land in the Somme.

"Anyone else hearing that?" Cole cocked his head to the side. "Am I crazy or is that an engine?"

Evan nodded. "No, there it is. Look." He pointed out through the narrow gap in the awning, and Cole craned his neck to get a look out the back. Off in the distance a beat up old red truck was rocketing across the parking lot towards the exit. It swerved wildly as it reached the street, almost skidding off the road before regaining traction.

The gunfire resumed, and everyone threw themselves to the floor once again. From the front of the truck what sounded like a half dozen rifles were firing, but it was clear the fleeing vehicle was well out of range of all but the luckiest of shots. An order was bellowed out over the gunfire, and a moment later the soldiers reappeared at the back of the truck.

"No touch," one ordered, raising his weapon as the others tossed pallets of food and water into the back. The folks at the back scrambled away as heavy boxes of tinned food landed painfully on top of them, and everyone huddled together at the front until the soldiers climbed in.

"We should have run," Evan whispered, taking a final longing look out the back of the truck before the awning was pinned down, sealing in the darkness. "I don't know how much more of this shit I can take."

The engine fired up, and with a jolt the truck began to move forward once again. In the stifling darkness of the truck Cole could hear only the rumbling engine, and a woman softly weeping.

•▾•

:::9:::

COLE SOMEHOW MANAGED to grab some rest. Unconsciousness, at least. The day had drained every last ounce of energy from him, and in the heat and darkness of the back of the truck the prisoners lay together in a dog pile, trying to find some kind of half comfortable position as the truck bounced along the potholed roads. Eventually, despite a pounding headache and a dull ache deep in his bones, the rumbling of the engine lulled Cole into fitful sleep.

It was hard to guess how long he slept. Could have been hours. Could have been just a few minutes. All Cole knew when he opened his eyes was that it was well after dark, and he felt rested. The truck was stopped, and the awning at the back had been flipped up. Beyond it a couple of the soldiers stood smoking casually, as if this were just a regular work day, and beyond them... beyond *them* the rest of the men were building what looked to be a makeshift internment camp, rolling out coils of barbed wire into some kind of enclosure.

The truck was parked in what looked like a public park that stretched out to the edge of the forest a ways off. In the center of the park stood a wooden gazebo, and around the edges of the manicured lawn stood folding tables that were being carelessly tossed aside as the soldiers cleared space. It took Cole a moment to notice it, but when he saw the colorful bunting hanging from the trees at the edge of the park he couldn't help but laugh at the absurdity of it all. One of the soldiers turned and shot him a warning glare, and he ducked his head.

"What is it?"

Cole turned and saw Evan pinned beneath several people, struggling to raise himself from the floor. He raised a finger to his lips and replied in a whisper.

"Looks like they're setting up some kind of camp. Lots of barbed wire." He thought about this for a moment. "Looks like they're planning to hold us prisoner, but I guess on the plus side at least it means they don't plan on killing us right away." He tried for a grin, but didn't quite manage it. "Every second we're alive is another second to plan our escape, right?"

"Any other Americans out there?"

Cole shook his head. "I don't see anyone else."

"Why do you think we're the only ones? Why keep us alive and shoot everyone else?"

Cole frowned. He'd been thinking about this for a while as the truck had been weaving across the miles of rough roads through the state. There was no doubt the Koreans had come across several other groups of people on the journey, but as far as they could tell from the back of the truck they'd all been either ignored or killed. The survivors from the airplane were the only ones still standing, and certainly the only group the soldiers had taken the trouble to capture.

"Insurance? Human shields, maybe? I don't know, it's the only thing that seems to make any sense. I can't figure out what the hell they're trying to do, but if they have some kind of goal in mind they must think it's worthwhile to keep some of us alive, and so long as I'm breathing I'm not in the mood to complain."

Evan sighed angrily. "I can't say I like that idea. What I wouldn't give for a gun right now. If I have to go out, I don't want to go out like a pussy."

Cole nodded. He felt exactly the same way. As a commercial pilot the thought of unexpected death was never far from his mind, and he'd always hoped that if he didn't have the good fortune to die at a hundred years old surrounded by loved ones he'd at least like to check out with some kind of *meaning*. The thought of a long, slow decline through illness or being wiped out in an RTA like a chump terrified him. He wanted to go out with a bang, not a whimper.

Hell, even dying on the flight deck of the downed 737 would have been a respectable death. At least there he'd have gone out like a man, trying to save the lives of his passengers. If his fate was to die at the hands of an enemy after sitting in the back of a truck like a sucker for hours on end, failing to fight back... well, he just prayed there really was an afterlife, because he'd want the opportunity to kick his own ass.

Evan narrowed his eyes. "What if we just rush them? You think it's possible?"

Cole considered it for a moment, then shook his head. "Not a chance. We have two right outside the truck and the rest about thirty yards away over open ground, most of them armed. We might take out the first two, but... no. Even if we take them and get their weapons the rest would just open up on the truck. There's no way we get to safety without losing people."

Cole jumped at the sudden sound of steel on steel. He looked around and saw one of the soldiers glaring into the truck, tapping the butt of his rifle against the back. The rest of the group began to stir as the soldier jerked his head to the side, gesturing for everyone to climb down.

Cole emerged first, eager to get the lay of the land. There wasn't much to see in the dark but he thought he could see a small parking lot at the edge of the park, a single old station wagon parked up close to the entrance. He assumed there must be a road on the other side of the lot, but at this distance it was little more than a guess. Off in the distance there seemed to be some sort of town or village, judging by the shapes of what looked like houses cast against the dim moonlight, but it was hard to be certain.

Up ahead the barbed wire enclosure seemed to be almost complete, a rough square around thirty meters to a side. Judging by its size Cole guessed that the survivors from the 737 weren't the only group of prisoners the soldiers intended to capture. He also guessed that they didn't give a damn about the conditions in which they were held, since the enclosure didn't contain so much as a shade tree or a latrine ditch. He suspected that meant they probably weren't planning to hold them for long. He didn't know if that was a good or bad sign, but so far he'd seen no reason for optimism.

The last of the group climbed down from the truck, and the guard behind them pushed them roughly into line against its side. He turned and called out a question to a soldier by the edge of the enclosure, an older man with the bearing of a leader, and the man called back. "*Set*," he said, holding up three fingers.

The soldier turned back to the truck and pointed to the three rightmost in the group, two men and a woman. "Come," he ordered, dragging the woman firmly by the arm. He led them to a spot in front of the leader and pushed them to their knees in a row.

Samantha began to weep, almost falling down but for Evan's arm supporting her weight. She'd been the fourth person in line, and she seemed well aware that had the soldier decided he needed one more she'd now be kneeling in front of him along with the rest. Cole had no idea what was about to happen to them, but he knew that nobody in the history of humanity had ever been lined up on their knees in front of armed men and come out the other side with a happy story.

The sound of an approaching engine came from somewhere on the other side of the truck, and moments later a set of headlights cast a long shadow on the grass at their feet. Cole frowned at the light, curious. It seemed to be casting an unusual shadow beneath the truck, and he carefully lowered himself until he could see its source.

"Evan," he whispered, standing up straight. "There's something under the truck just behind your feet. You think you can pull it out without drawing attention?"

Evan glanced down between his legs, trying to get a look. "What is it?"

"I've no idea. Probably nothing, but it can't hurt to check. If they're really dumb they might be hiding a few guns under there."

Evan narrowed his eyes and scanned the park.

Most of the men were busy laying down the barbed wire, and the rest were focused on the leader and the row of civilians kneeling before him. Nobody seemed to be paying much attention to the rest of the prisoners, so Evan slowly lowered himself to one knee and pretended to tie his shoelace. With his free leg he reached back and hooked his shoe around the object beneath the truck, and with a few soft nudges he managed to bring it close enough to reach with a hand.

It was a small wooden box. Not the kind of sturdy, heavy duty crate you'd expect from the military, but the sort of cheap unfinished pine boxes on sale for fifteen bucks at Walmart, held together with flimsy tacks and dowels. As Evan raised himself to his feet he gave it a light kick with the toe of his boot, flipping the lid to the ground.

Cole looked down at the crate, squinting in the darkness, and he could barely believe his eyes. "Are those fireworks?"

Tightly packed in polystyrene peanuts were several dozen rockets, a few packs of firecrackers and a handful of Roman candles, and beside them all was a small trigger start propane torch and a box of matches.

"What the hell are these guys doing with a crate of fireworks?"

Cole thought about it for a moment before he

finally made the connection, and as soon as he did he felt dumb for taking so long to figure it out. "It's not the Koreans. Look at the bunting in the trees. Look at those tables at the edge of the park. I think someone was planning a July Fourth firework display tonight."

Evan shook his head in disbelief. "So what, this is just luck? You think these guys just happened to park right on top of a crate of fireworks by random chance?"

"Luck. God. George Washington's ghost. Who knows? All I know is it might give us a chance to get the hell out of here."

"How do you mean?"

Cole began to speak, but at that moment the approaching vehicle finally arrived in the park, skidding to a halt a little ahead of the troop truck. It was an old Humvee, painted in tan, and Cole froze as the doors opened and three soldiers emerged. A moment later a middle aged man was dragged by his elbow from the back seat.

"Get your damned hands off me, you sonofabitch!" the man yelled, trying to shake off the soldier's grip. Even in the dim light Cole could see that his nose was broken, and a stream of blood glistened from a wound on his temple.

The soldier who appeared to be in charge waited patiently as the man was dragged towards him and dumped roughly to the ground in front of the three survivors from the plane. For a long moment he surveyed the new arrival, seemingly amused by his anger, and with a curt nod he gave the order to have him silenced. The soldier beside him took his rifle and gave the man a firm crack on the back of his head with the butt. Not enough to knock him out, but more than enough to send him sprawling to the ground.

"Get on your feet."

It took Cole a moment to realize the order had come from the leader. His English was crisp and clear, with a heavy Korean accent.

The American was pulled to his feet, swaying a little and clutching his head. The soldier ignored his obvious pain and continued to speak.

"You are the sheriff of this town, yes?"

The man shook his head, doing his best to draw himself up to his full height. "We don't have a sheriff. I'm the chief of police, Chuck Roberts."

The soldier nodded. "And where is your mayor? My men tell me you refuse to help them locate him." He reached into his pocket and withdrew a small notebook, flipping through the pages for a moment. "A Mr. Joseph Burnham. That's the name of your mayor, yes?" He pronounced the name Burn Ham.

The chief of police nodded. "Yeah, that's his name, and like I was telling your men I don't have the first Goddamned clue where he is, and I wouldn't tell you if I did."

For a long, uncomfortable moment the soldier silently studied the chief. Eventually he nodded, let out a small, disappointed sigh, and then in one smooth motion pulled his revolver from its holster, took a smart step forward, leveled the barrel at the back of the head of the first man on his knees and pulled the trigger. The man slumped forward, lifeless, and beside him the two others began to weep and tremble.

The chief froze in shock, stunned into silence by the barbaric act, and the soldier lowered the gun to his waist.

"Now you will tell me where I can find your mayor."

"I don't know!" the chief insisted, his bravado completely evaporated. "Please don't shoot anyone! I promise you I don't know where Burnham is. I haven't seen him for hours!" He balled up his fists as the soldier took another step forward and raised his gun once again. "No, please don't. Please, just – Please! *For God's sake, don't –*"

The gun fired again, but this time the target had begun to run. He pulled himself to his feet, but he didn't make it two steps before falling to the ground, a bullet in his back. A second shot finished him off.

"Oh, God damn you, you evil bastard." Now the chief was in tears. "You'll burn in Hell for this."

The soldier sighed. "Must I shoot this woman, or

will you tell me where I can find your mayor?" His voice was almost drowned out by the hysterical crying of the woman at his feet. Her hands were clasped together in prayer, and she let out a panicked squeal as she heard him take a step forward behind her.

"Wait!" the chief yelled, holding up both hands in pleading. "I'll take you to him. I promise I'll take you to him, just please, please leave her alone. Please, for the love of God, let her live."

The soldier nodded. "You will accompany my men to his location directly. No delays. No tricks. Your mayor will be here to formally surrender to me within thirty minutes, of there will be consequences."

The chief nodded eagerly. "Yes, OK, yes. I'll go find him right away, no problem." He began to turn back towards the Humvee, but froze as he saw the soldier raise his arm. "No!"

The revolver barked. The woman fell forward, her voice silenced and her prayers unanswered.

"That was the price of your hesitation and your treachery, Chief Roberts." He waved his hand in the direction of the truck. "If you fail to return with your leader the executions will continue. We have..."

He paused, frowning.

The prisoners next to the truck were nowhere to be seen.

•▼•

:::10:::

COLE CROUCHED BESIDE the Humvee, desperately trying to stop his heart from pounding as he pulled open the rear door. The closest soldier was right on the other side of the vehicle and just a few yards ahead, well within earshot if he made more than a whisper of sound.

He clicked the trigger of the propane torch just as the third prisoner was shot, masking the sound with the echo of the report. His eyes filled with tears as he saw the woman slump to the ground, but he knew he couldn't afford to be distracted. There were still seven of the group left alive, and if this didn't work they'd all be dead soon enough.

The timing was crucial. It had been years since he'd lit fireworks, but he guessed that the fuses on the rockets and Roman candles would burn for around ten seconds before ignition. He hoped his guess was halfway accurate, because he needed that time to get back to the truck.

On the rear seat of the Humvee he set down a row of two dozen rockets with the words 'Uncle Sam's Revenge' printed on the tubes, making sure the fuses were ready to light before he pulled the row of firecrackers from over his shoulder. He stood up as much as he dared, peering though the windows to catch a glimpse of Evan about thirty yards away on the opposite side of the truck, skulking in the darkness on hands and knees. He couldn't see him at first, but when he lifted the propane torch to the window – the signal to begin – he could just about make out a waving arm, just a moving shape in the darkness.

Cole took a deep breath, whispering a final prayer as he brought the blue flame of the torch to the fuses of the firecrackers. With one smooth movement he lit them all, and then tossed them like a Frisbee as far as he could manage, deep into the trees at the edge of the park. He paused for a moment to ensure nobody had noticed him and then lit the fuses of the rockets, dropping the still lit propane torch on the back seat before gently closing the door.

The Koreans had finally noticed that they'd vanished from beside the truck. Instantly their rifles were raised and trained on the vehicle, and Cole could do nothing but pray they wouldn't fire. Samantha had taken the rest of the survivors to the back, and he wasn't confident they'd survive a barrage of bullets through the canvas.

His prayers were answered as the row of firecrackers began to explode in the trees. Every last soldier spun towards the sound as Cole began to run back towards the truck, and in the darkness he could see the fuses Evan had lit glowing. He reached the back of the truck just as a group of four soldiers reached the Humvee. One pulled open the driver's door just as the rockets inside began to fire off, and he fell backward, alarmed, as fireworks ricocheted wildly through the vehicle and began to shoot out towards him.

As Cole reached the back of the truck he saw Evan sprinting just ahead of his own fireworks, a long row of ten shot repeater Roman candles he'd pushed into the ground at angle, all of them facing the soldier in command. The man himself was focused on the firecrackers, crouching behind the body of one of the men he'd shot, but as the assault came from the rear he turned with a look of shock, just as Evan tackled him at the waist.

"Run!" Evan yelled at the chief of police, pinning the soldier to the ground. "Get to the truck!"

The chief backed away uncertainly as Evan began to rain down violent, uncontrolled blows on the soldier's face. In the madness Cole could barely see him, but he could tell his friend had lost it. He pummeled the soldier mercilessly, throwing everything he had into each punch, and Cole knew he wouldn't stop until the man was dead.

"Damn it!" he cursed, pushing himself from the

back of the truck and running back towards Evan. As he passed the chief of police he yelled at him, "You're driving! Keys are in the ignition!" He didn't stop to see if the man followed his order. There was no time. Already the soldiers had turned back from the firecrackers and noticed what was going on behind them. The distraction had bought them time, but it was over.

"Evan!" Cole grabbed him by the shoulder, and immediately Evan turned and tried to attack, without a clue who he was attacking. Cole easily blocked the swinging forearm of his older, smaller friend and held his shoulder tight until he stopped struggling. "It's over!" he yelled, looking down at the bloodied figure Evan had left on the ground. "Let's go!"

Evan allowed himself to be pulled from the ground just as the engine of the truck roared into life, and Cole waved to the chief as they ran towards the back. "Drive! Drive!" They reached the back just as the truck began to move, and Cole jumped up to the footplate, took Evan's hand and pulled him up beside him.

Behind them the soldiers had begun firing on the truck, but it was no use. They were still blinded by the Roman candles firing towards them, barely able to see the truck in the fractions of a second between each new blast. The Humvee was already burning on the inside, the propane torch catching the fabric of the rear seats. As the truck bounced through the parking lot and swerved onto the road the small, terrified group inside held each other's hands in prayer, thanking God for allowing them to survive.

"Is everyone OK?" Cole asked, climbing fully inside the truck and closing the flap behind him. There were nods all around, along with a few grateful smiles. Samantha climbed to her feet and clutched Evan in a tight embrace, and Cole felt his cheeks flush as she deeply kissed him. It was an open secret that Evan's wife had left him when she discovered he was having an affair with a colleague, but Cole had never broached the subject and Evan was far too private a person to talk about it.

"Where are we going?" one of the surviving men asked.

Cole shrugged. "For now I guess we're going wherever the chief of police wants to drive us. I'm hoping it's far away. We'll have a talk as soon as it's safe to pull over." He turned to Evan, thankful to see he'd broken from his embrace with Samantha. "Evan, lemme take a look at those hands. I wouldn't be surprised if you'd broken something with all those—" He froze. "Evan?"

Evan's face was deathly pale. Almost gray, as if every drop of his blood had been drained. As Cole watched he reached his hand down to his leg, and when he pulled it away it glistened red.

"Oh," he murmured, his voice weak. "Oh no."

His legs gave way beneath him, and as he tumbled to the floor of the truck Samantha began to scream.

•▼•

:::11:::

3AM
BEYOND WILLOW FALLS

"SHOULD... UMMM... DO you think we should stop her?"

Shepherd sat on the open tailgate of Big Joe's truck, smoking a Marlboro from the stash Joe had tucked away beneath his supplies, and he watched sympathetically as the young woman from the truck struggled to dig a grave with the small folding shovel Shepherd had packed to dig latrine pits. It was barely larger than a trowel. It would take her hours to dig a hole large enough for the dead pilot.

Cole shook his head. "I think she needs the distraction." He gratefully took a cigarette offered by Joe, nodding with gratitude. "She and Evan had a thing going on. Best to let her focus on something, you know? Better than sitting here dwelling on it." He lit the cigarette, took a deep pull and coughed. "Oh hell," he croaked, passing the cigarette back to Joe. "I quit ten years ago, and now I remember why."

Shepherd looked beyond the young flight

attendant scrabbling at the ground to the town below, a mile away at the foot of the hill. The gas station fire was finally burning itself out, and in the blackness below the only thing visible was a set of dim headlights in the distance, somewhere near the suburbs on the wealthier side of town. Shepherd kept his eyes on it, ready to grab his gun if the vehicle made a move towards them.

Big Joe stood on the tailgate and peered towards the cab of the troop truck, the interior dimly lit by the overhead light. "What you got, Chuck?"

"Hang on," the chief replied, clumsily lowering himself backwards from the truck. He jogged over to them, a manila folder in his hands and a rifle slung over his shoulder. "Found this gun behind the driver's seat, plus a fair bit of ammo. Oh, and this." He passed the folder to Joe.

Joe flipped through the bulging folder, slipping out pages as he went. "Looks like... umm... OK, looks like the title for the truck. Registered to something called the Shin Han Holding Company out of Richmond." He flipped through more pages. "Huh, there's a half dozen of them here, all registered to the same company. The truck, two Humvees and a few Willys Jeeps... And look at this. Some of these things were registered four, five years ago. You think they've been planning this that long?"

Shepherd took a sheaf of paper from Joe and

flipped through the pages. He stopped on a vehicle title that registered the transfer of ownership from a Wisconsin auction house in 2015. "I guess this explains how they had vehicles ready to go right away. Makes more sense than airdropping them in if you can just buy the damned things and make sure they're protected from an EMP. Hey, I wonder if—"

"What in the everloving hell?" Joe jumped down from the tailgate clutching a sheaf of papers. "I warned them it was a bad idea! I screamed bloody murder, but they went ahead and did it anyway!"

Shepherd tossed his cigarette butt and stood. "Woah, woah, settle down, Joe. What is it?"

"It's the God damned register!" He slammed the papers down on the tailgate and began to pace angrily. "They got hold of the damned thing. All our names! The whole damned list!"

Shepherd was thoroughly confused, but as he looked down at the crumpled sheet at the top of the sheaf it all began to make sense.

Virginia Registry of Firearms – Campbell County.

It was a long alphabetical list of names and addresses, beside each of them a set of short codes. Shepherd quickly flipped through the stack until he found the S section, and sure enough there was his own name and address. Beside it were the letters PASx1, SAPx1 and SARx1, and at the bottom of the page was a key.

PAS: Pump action shotgun

SAP: Semi-automatic pistol

SAR: Semi-automatic rifle

Shepherd remembered the protests about the state register in the summer of 2018. Big Joe and the chief had masterminded a public awareness campaign, begging the locals to call their Congressman and tell him they were dead against it, but it had done no good.

The proposal had come in the wake of a spate of mass shootings within a half hour drive of Richmond, four of them in just two months, one of them in a high school that resulted in the deaths of six promising and extremely popular young football players, and against all odds it had managed to ride the wave of public shock and pass the General Assembly.

By January 1st of 2019 all firearms of any kind were required to be registered with the state, and all gun owners needed to provide a set of fingerprints and a current address. Concealed carry permits were switched from shall issue to may issue, and for the first time in Virginia open carry required a permit – a separate permit for each weapon – only approved after evidence of registration was presented. The penalty for non-compliance with any of the new laws was a hefty fine and the threat of a few months of jail time.

The raft of new laws seemed designed not so much to prevent shootings as to make owning a gun as inconvenient as humanly possible. Collectors needed to complete dozens or even hundreds of application forms just to stay on the right side of the law, and gun owners couldn't even legally visit a shooting range without providing evidence of compliance.

Big Joe had been the loudest opponent of the register in Willow Falls, but of course almost everyone in Campbell County thought it was a bad idea. Joe had argued – fairly logically – that a simple register of firearms would do little to stop gun violence, since it would do nothing to keep guns out of the hands of irresponsible or dangerous owners, and would only caused inconvenience for the good guys, but his warnings fell on deaf ears. Despite the vocal opposition the state pushed ahead regardless, and in the year since most gun owners in Virginia had reluctantly fallen in line.

"You think they've been targeting people using this?" The chief asked, searching for his own name on the list.

"You're damned right I do!" Joe fumed, grabbing the stack of pages out of his hands. "Chuck, you were in town when it all started. Did they hit everyone, or just the houses with lots of guns?"

The chief ran his palm across his stubble, deep in

thought, and winced as he accidentally brushed a finger against his broken nose. "Well, I guess it's hard to say. Can't say I saw all that much from the back of the Hummer, but I know they hit the Andersons. And Hunt's place. And I'm pretty sure they got Jack Patton out at his farm."

Joe nodded, flipping the pages. "Anderson, Hunt, Patton. All of them have enough weapons to supply an army. Damned Koreans are trying a surgical strike!"

The chief shook his head in disbelief. "That makes no sense. How the heck do they think they could pull that off? They can't just roll in, kill a few folks and declare themselves the winners. Almost everyone's got guns, right? Everyone'll fight back."

Shepherd spoke up, trying to dredge up stats from a half remembered article he'd once read. "No, not really. Around here we probably have more than most, but not everyone in the country lives like we do. There may be as many guns as there are people in the US, but only about a quarter of Americans actually *own* a gun. Most of those who do only have one or two, but when it comes down to it around half of all the privately owned guns in the US belong to just three percent of the people. Our civilian firepower is *insanely* concentrated. You've seen Jack Patton's arsenal, right? Hell, he could open his own gun store out there at the farm. The guy must have two hundred weapons but he's only got one pair of hands, and when it comes to a straight firefight he's no greater a threat than someone who only owns a single weapon."

Abi chimed in. "That's right. We like to think that every last man, woman and child in the country would take up arms against an invading army, but how many of us are *really* ready to fight? Only one in four of us even owns a gun. Even fewer than that really know how to handle a weapon in a combat situation, and even fewer than *that* both know how to shoot and are ready to take a life. Think about Vietnam and WWII. How many of those soldiers ever actually killed anyone?"

Shepherd nodded in agreement as Abi continued. "Military literature is full of suggestions – some based on suspect evidence, to be fair – that only a small minority of soldiers on the battlefield ever pull the trigger, with examples going back as far as the Great War. It doesn't seem to matter how much training the soldiers have been through, how much combat they've seen or even how much danger they're in. Few ever fire their weapons, and many of those who do don't try to hit the enemy."

The chief butted in. "Yeah, I think I heard about that. Killology, right? That's what they call the study of the... you know, the psychology of combat soldiers or whatever? It's all about fight or flight, and that other stuff."

"Fight, flight, posture or submit," Abi nodded. "You all know about fight or flight, I'm guessing? When a soldier is faced with a threat he can either fight or run, but those aren't his only options. He can also submit to the enemy. He can tap out of the fight and surrender, hopefully ending up in a POW camp that isn't staffed by monsters. That option isn't much used today, now that most of the enemies we fight aren't exactly subscribers to *Geneva Conventions Monthly*." Her eyes rested for a moment on the body of Evan, the pilot.

"And then there's the final option: posture. They can pretend to fight. They can go through the motions, poke their head out from cover and maybe even blindly fire off a few rounds, but as far as efficacy goes they're pretty much the kid on the football field who makes a lot of noise but always makes sure he's exactly where the ball isn't."

She seemed to catch herself, for the first time realizing that she might be addressing veterans who may not appreciate this theory. "Don't get me wrong, it's not that these men are cowards, or even that they're frozen by fear. There are lots of theories as to why so few soldiers fire their weapons in combat, but a popular one is simply that the act of leveling a gun at the enemy, squeezing the trigger and intentionally taking the life of a fellow human being is much more difficult that it looks in the movies. Murder isn't clean, and it's almost never quick. It's bloody, visceral and gruesome, and it's an act that forever changes the person holding the weapon. It's just not in the nature of most people to kill. The military spends billions training soldiers to be able to do it without falling to pieces."

Shepherd nodded. "Exactly. So how would civilians measure up? How would accountants, farmers, lawyers and baristas perform against an enemy they never expected to face? If only a small fraction of soldiers can bring themselves to kill even after months or years of physical and psychological training, how could Ted at the auto parts store manage to fight off an invasion?"

"You know, they could actually pull this off," he said, keeping his voice low, as if it was heresy to suggest that America could ever be conquered. "Think about it. They use the EMP to knock us back to the Stone Age when we least expect it, destroying our civilian and military infrastructure with a single blow. They take out the President and everyone around him in the confusion, shattering the chain of command into a million pieces. Then, just when we're all reeling, they swoop in and kill the greatest threats they face, the heavily armed folks who've been preparing for years for just this kind of thing. And then they top it all off by capturing our leaders – they wanted you for a reason, Joe, and I'm pretty sure it wasn't for your basketball skills."

He turned to the town below, just now beginning to emerge from the darkness as the pre-dawn light cast a ghostly blue across the landscape. "Hell, maybe they won't succeed, but they *could*. They have us on the ropes."

Abi followed Shepherd's gaze towards the town. "So what do we do now?"

Shepherd pondered the question for a moment, and for the life of him he couldn't think of a good angle. The Koreans had them outflanked and outgunned. They could have been preparing this attack for *years*, hiding in plain sight, gathering supplies and steeling themselves for the day they finally took America out. Shepherd was on the back foot. Hell, *America* was on the back foot, reeling from a sucker punch and just trying to stay on its feet. How could they possibly...

"Hey, Joe," he said, a thought suddenly occurring to him, "check that register again. Do you see Arno Novak's name on it?"

Joe flipped to the Ns and ran a finger down the pages, his brow knitting as he realized the name was absent. "Well, son of a bitch. He told me he wasn't gonna register his guns, but I thought he was just talking out his ass."

Shepherd nodded. He knew Arno Novak about as

well as anyone else in Willow Falls did, which is to say not that well at all, but he knew that if Novak said he wouldn't put up with shit from no *gubmint heavies* he damned well meant it.

"OK then, we have a plan" he said, standing from the tailgate of Joe's truck. "First we help Samantha and Cole bury their friend."

"And then?" Abi asked..

Shepherd picked up his Mossberg, pushed it into his bag and swung it over his shoulder. "Then we go get ourselves enough guns to take out these bastards."

•▼•

:::**12**:::

THE SUN WAS just about breaking over the distant hills as Shepherd's Jeep reached the hidden turnoff. He pulled in to the side of the road about fifty yards back and killed the engine. Shepherd only knew the turnoff was there because he'd been called out regularly on noise complaints filed by Novak's closest neighbor, an elderly woman who lived a half mile from the house who didn't appreciate being awoken by gunfire every morning at dawn.

Arno Novak was an *intensely* private man. He was the kind of guy who only interacted with other people on his own terms, and he didn't encourage or even tolerate visitors to his home. In fact, he kept the entrance to his driveway camouflaged with loose foliage to blend in with the surrounding forest, and he even made a habit of carefully sweeping away his tire tracks in the dirt after he entered or departed, just to make sure nobody could guess that a vehicle may have passed that way.

Novak was... well, if there had ever been a resident of Willow Falls more paranoid than Shep's own father it was Arno Novak. Novak trusted nothing and nobody. Like Shep Senior he believed that the end of society was always right around the corner, but where Shep's father had believed the end would come at the hands of a foreign enemy Novak was certain that the real danger was the enemy within: the US government.

Novak had been born in Willow Falls a few years after the end of World War Two, the first and only member of his family born on American soil. His parents had been Ashkenazi Jews who'd fled their native Czechoslovakia in 1936 when they'd seen the writing on the wall, realizing sooner than most that the worst was yet to come, and they'd left behind dozens of family members and countless friends among the three hundred fifty thousand strong Jewish population in the old country. They'd spent every last penny they had crossing Europe, and they'd boarded a ship bound for the US with little more than the clothes on their backs.

Of course their fear had proved to be justified, and then some. By the time the Novaks finally gained their American citizenship in the year of Arno's birth there were fewer than twenty thousand Jews left alive in Czechoslovakia. Today, as Novak never failed to remind anyone within earshot whenever he raised the subject, there were only three thousand in the modern Czech Republic.

Young Arno had grown up on a rich diet of all the

most horrific stories of the old country. He'd been told of the impoverished and starving ghettos that appeared all throughout Europe, and the herding of people like him and his parents into them. He'd been told of the tightening grip of the Nazis over the lives of the people, both Jewish and Gentile alike. He'd been told of the capitulation of the governments of neighboring countries in the face of sweeping fascism, and of the final dark days before his parents fled the continent, pleading with their family to join them but finding their pleas rebuffed with the usual dismissive, blind optimism. *It will all be fine. Don't worry, sanity will prevail. You're worrying about nothing. They won't let it continue like this.*

They. They were the governments and institutions that allowed themselves to be swept up and drowned beneath totalitarian rule. *They* were the people who proved too weak to resist, to fight back in the name of freedom, and who had allowed Novak's family to be slaughtered through their inaction. *They* were to be despised, resisted and feared, because it was only their cowardice that had allowed it all to happen.

Even the happiest of stories from Novak's childhood had been tainted by death, tragedy and betrayal. Uncle Levi was a skilled cellist, the pride of Dubnica, and on his way to a first chair in the Prague Symphony. *Oh, Arno, you would have adored his music. It was like God himself played through him.*

He died in a rail car on the way to Treblinka, the poor man. Arno's aunt was known as a great beauty, courted as a young woman by the men of all the finest families in Bratislava. *But of course her beauty couldn't save her in Auschwitz,* his parents would say.

The tragic tales of Novak's lost family and stolen heritage had imbued in him from an early age a seam of mistrust in government that ran so deep in his heart that there was precious little room for anything else. In every story, in every creased and faded photograph, in every small memento his parents had managed to save as they fled, he saw the evidence of what happened when regular people allowed their leaders too much power. He saw what happened when governments were hijacked by evil.

Shepherd would have no way of knowing any of this were it not for the fact that it was all Novak ever talked about whenever he ventured into town. At least twice a month since Shepherd had been a child Novak had spent the day sitting at the counter of the diner with the papers spread out in front of him, drinking endless refills of black coffee and angrily holding court with anyone willing to listen about the latest outrages of the government, likening them to developments in pre-war Europe. Novak was a walking example of Godwin's Law, a man who could shoehorn the Nazis into a conversation about cupcakes.

Democrat or Republican, politicians were all the same to him. He didn't care about political parties. In fact he didn't seem to hold any recognizable political positions at all, apart from the fervent belief that all politicians were devious snakes who'd gleefully break ground on new concentration camps if it took them a step closer towards achieving their goals.

Shepherd rattled off to Cole and Abi a condensed version of Novak's story in an effort to prepare them for what was to come, and Joe nodded along as he spoke. When he was done Abi frowned.

"Wait... if this Novak guy hates all politicians, why's Joe here?" She touched him on the shoulder. "Sorry, Joe, no offense."

"None taken, darling," Joe grinned. "The truth is that old Arno always gave me a pass. He doesn't believe I'm a real politician, you see, because... well, because I'm a little person." He shrugged. "I know, I know, it makes no sense, but you can't expect much sense from an angry old coot who lives out in the woods. He thinks people elected me mayor as a goof, and in his book that means I stopped a *real* politician running the town. Couple years back he even tried to convince me to run for President."

"And you're OK with that? Isn't it a little insulting?"

Joe let out a laugh. "Well sure it is, but I give *him* a

pass. See, that crazy old codger won me my first election. Nobody even knew my name until he started talking about me. I couldn't even afford to pay for lawn signs, but there was old Novak sitting in the diner, spending his days trying to convince everyone to vote for me as a protest, like a 'none of the above' candidate, a sort of Paddy Chayefsky thing. Y'know, 'I'm mad as hell, and I'm not gonna take this anymore'? And God bless him, it worked."

Shepherd grinned. "He's not wrong, you know. I'd never even bothered to vote in a mayoral election until Novak started his little pro-Burnham campaign in the diner. I didn't know any of his policies. I just knew I was sick to the back teeth of the last guy."

Joe nodded. "Yup. In any case, it's Shep here who should be worried. What does Arno call the cops, Shep? The jackbooted..."

"The jackbooted enforcers of the fascist regime, and the amoral, mercenary gun hand of the state." He gave Abi a grin. "Yeah, he can be a little intense." He checked his watch, turned to the rising sun and sighed. "OK, I guess we should make a move. We need to catch him before he goes out hunting."

Shepherd climbed from the truck and turned back to the rear door, shaking his head as Cole emerged with Shepherd's Ruger in hand. "No, no guns. Novak will shoot you dead if he sees that."

Cole's face turned white, and he tossed the gun to

the back seat like it was a live snake. Big Joe pulled his Sig Sauer from his holster and placed it in the glove box, grinning as he noticed Cole's expression. "Don't worry, kid, Shep's just kidding." Cole relaxed a little, and a relieved smile crept onto his stricken face.

"Yeah, I am," Shepherd confirmed, walking towards the hidden entrance to Novak's driveway. "He'd just put one in your leg."

It took five minutes before Shepherd found a way through the thick foliage to reach the entrance. This part of the forest had been planted with a mixture of thorn bushes, stinging nettles and poison ivy, no doubt Novak's doing, and while it would be easy to move aside the branches Novak used to block the main entrance Shepherd was concerned there might be a nasty surprise waiting for anyone who tried to enter that way without an invite.

"Follow in my footsteps, and keep an eye out for booby traps," he said, finally finding a way through the thick undergrowth.

"Booby traps?" Abi stopped directly behind him, suddenly tense.

"Yeah. Bear traps, trip wires, punji sticks, that kind of thing. I'm not saying we'll find any, but I wouldn't put it past him. Hold up, I can see the gate." He pushed on through the dense, spiky foliage, feeling the thorns scratch against his legs, and he finally reached the wide steel gate that blocked the driveway. He laughed uneasily as he noticed the two signs attached to it.

If you can read this, I already have you in my sights.

Forget the dog... Beware the owner.

"Charming," muttered Abi, shielding herself behind Shepherd as if she expected sniper fire to break through the trees at any moment.

Shepherd reached for the latch. "Don't worry, I'm sure it's just – *Ow! Motherf—*"

"What is it?!" Big Joe rushed forward as Shepherd snatched his hand away.

"The damned thing's electrified!"

"Shit, are you OK?"

Shepherd nodded, shaking his hand and leaning in to examine the latch. "Yeah, I'm fine, it's just one of those little four volt Yellow Jackets the cattle farmers use." He leaned over the other side of the fence, careful not to touch anything, and hidden behind the gatepost he saw the small battery powered black and yellow box attached to the other side. "Didn't really hurt, but it surprised the crap out of me. Jesus, of all the things to survive an EMP. We lose the lights and the AC, but this damned pain box comes through without a scratch. Where's the justice?"

"Ummm... guys?" Cole took a step forward. "I think I see movement up there." He pointed up the driveway, where Novak's house was just visible through the trees.

"Arno?" Shepherd yelled at the top of his voice. "Arno, it's Shep and Mayor Burnham. You home?"

For a few minutes they waited nervously, hands out of their pockets and standing as non-threateningly as possible, until finally something began to move through the trees. Cole and Abi shrank back as a figure emerged from the undergrowth and walked cautiously towards the gate. A man of around seventy, tall and wiry, with a neglected head of white hair pulled back into a lazy ponytail and a beard that looked like it hadn't been trimmed since Christmas. He was wearing nothing but a threadbare terrycloth robe and a pair of slippers, and in one hand he carried a flask lid full of steaming coffee. Nestled in the crook of his free arm was an antique Winchester Model 94.

"OK, how'd you find out?" he asked, his voice dripping with suspicion.

"Find out what?" Shepherd asked, confused.

Novak took a sip of his coffee before answering. "What, you got spies in the woods or something. You been surveilling me, Officer Shepherd? Come on, how'd you find out?"

Big Joe took a step forward and nodded a greeting at Novak. "Morning, Arno. Find out about what? Shep here don't know what you're talking about, and to be honest I'm a little confused too."

Novak narrowed his eyes for a moment, looking for a hint of subterfuge, a tell in Joe's expression. Finally he sighed, reached for the Yellow Jacket and flipped the switch, shutting off the electric fence. He pointed towards Cole and Abi. "Can't say I warm to strangers at the homestead."

Joe nodded. "I vouch for them, Arno, you can take my word. We've all come correct. Left our firearms in the truck."

Novak nodded brusquely, swinging open the gate and jerking his chin towards the house. "In any case they'll have to wait here. That OK with you, Joe?"

Joe turned to Cole and Abi. Both of them nodded enthusiastically. "I'd say that'll be fine."

"Then I suppose you better come see him."

"See who?" Shepherd was beginning to lose patience. It was far too early for riddles, and he hadn't had nearly enough sleep for this.

"Who do you think?" Novak replied. "The damned gook soldier."

•▼•

:::**13**:::

NOVAK'S HOUSE LOOKED like a wreck from the outside, a collapsing pile that seemed as if it had been hammered together from salvaged driftwood. The splintered boards of the front wall were covered in moss and bird droppings, and the porch that wrapped around the property looked like it would collapse entirely with the lightest footstep, but Shep knew that inside the house was perfectly comfortable. Novak didn't give a damn about outward appearances, but he was no spartan. Through the window Shepherd caught a glimpse of a stone fireplace, and beyond that a clean and well-equipped kitchen. Novak hunted and grew almost everything he ate, and Shepherd knew he kept his kitchen so clean it would easily pass the most stringent restaurant health inspection.

The shed, on the other hand...

Novak led them past the house to the shed, a sprawling garage-cum-workshop where he kept his truck and dressed his kills before taking the meat to the freezer. Apart from a few modern security measures the shed really was a piece of crap, a tumbledown mass of rickety boards so knotted that a child could climb through the gaps without even opening the door. Novak swung open the side door with a creak, and as he ducked into the murky darkness Shepherd followed, flinching a little as he felt the tickle of a cobweb on his forehead.

"What's going on here, Arno?" Shepherd asked, but as soon as he spoke he heard the sound of low, steady breathing. He fell silent. In the darkness at the other end of the shed beyond Novak's truck someone was asleep, or at least passed out.

Novak turned on a small battery powered LED lantern, casting a light that didn't so much illuminate the shed as create a dozen eerie shadows against the walls. "Found him skulking around near the Anderson place sometime yes'day. Damned fool got himself separated from the group, and I was kind enough to lend a helping hand."

Shepherd could see what Novak meant by 'helping hand' as soon as he rounded the truck and caught a look at the prisoner. It was a young Asian man in camo fatigues, maybe in his mid twenties, his arms and legs tightly bound with fencing wire to a steel chair. His nose was obviously broken, and to Shepherd's untrained eye he had what looked to be a broken orbital bone. His right eye was swollen closed, and his cheek looked almost dented. His mouth was covered with a strip of silver duct tape.

Beyond the beating he'd taken the young man's

left trouser leg had been torn up to the knee, and around it a bandage had been wrapped around a wound that had gone uncleaned. The skin around the bandage was tacky and red with dried blood.

"You shot him?"

"Well, what do you think? Damned right I shot him," replied Novak, as if it was the dumbest question he'd ever heard. He nodded to a box over in a dark corner of the shed. "I've got my shortwave. I heard what's going on."

Big Joe emerged around the front of the truck and sighed angrily. "Damn it, Arno, what the hell do you think you're doing taking prisoners? It's not like he'll be able to tell you anything."

Novak chuckled. "Oh, he told me plenty, believe me."

"He speaks English?" Shepherd cringed as he noticed beside the chair a plastic soda bottle half full of water, and beside that a rag. "You waterboarded him?" he asked, hoping he was jumping to conclusions.

"Among other things. Didn't take much to soften him up." He grabbed the bottle up from the floor and emptied a little over the face of the prisoner, who came to almost immediately, spluttering and jerking his head from side to side to escape the stream. Novak reached down and grabbed a loose corner of the duct tape, yanking it quickly from the young man's face.

"Stop, please!" he yelled. "I told you everything!"

The young man shook his head as Novak stopped pouring the water. He opened the one bloodshot eye that wasn't swollen closed, and as soon as he saw Shepherd and Joe he tried to jump from his chair, held back only by the fencing wire. The legs screeched across the concrete floor like fingernails down a chalkboard.

"Please help me! He's torturing me! Please get me out of here! I'll go to jail! Anywhere!"

"You shut your damned mouth," Novak ordered, leaning in close, "unless you want a bullet in the other leg."

Shepherd turned to Joe, his mouth hanging open with shock. The kid spoke with a strong American accent. West coast. California, maybe. If not for the camo fatigues he might not have seemed out of place riding the surf at Huntington Beach.

"What the hell?"

Novak nodded. "Yeah, tell me about it." He reached into a pocket of his robe and withdrew a passport and ID card, tossing them both to Shepherd. "Philippines passport and a Marymount college ID. He's got a student visa that expired four years ago, and he was stamped into the country in 2011. Didn't take long for him to admit the passport's a fake. This kid sure as hell ain't from Manila."

"Did you say 2011?"

"Uh huh. Heard on the shortwave that some of these guys have been airdropped in, but according to this little punk that was just the commanders. Most of the foot soldiers have been here for years, digging themselves in like ticks, just waiting for the go order."

"I'm sorry! I'm so sorry! I didn't want to do this! I love America! They—"

The slap came without warning, so hard that the chair rocked on its back legs for a moment before rattling back to the ground. A pale mark appeared on the young man's cheek, quickly replaced with a burning hand print as the blood rushed back to the skin. He closed his mouth and quietly whimpered, but there were no tears. He looked like he'd run dry of tears hours ago.

Joe raised a hand as Novak pulled back to hit him again. "Arno, no! I want to hear what the kid has to say." He stepped forward, meeting the kid at eye level. "What do you mean you didn't want to do this?"

The young man spoke in a shaky voice, clearly in pain. "My family... they have my family. You don't know what it's like!"

"Who has your family?"

The young man met Joe's gaze and set his jaw. "The... the government. The regime back home. If we don't do as they say they'll... My family isn't safe."

"Oh, I've heard enough of this crap," Novak

growled. "He'll say anything to get outta that chair."

Joe shook his head. "Well now, wait a minute, Arno, let's not jump to conclusions here. Kid says he's under duress, and he might just be telling the truth. Let's at least stop hitting him."

"I don't care if they have his dear old momma at gunpoint, Joe," Arno replied, angrily. "You didn't see what I saw."

"What do you mean? What did you see?"

Novak turned to the prisoner, clenching his fists. He spoke through gritted teeth. "Do you wanna tell them, or should I?"

The young man whimpered softly, rolling his head back and forth as if he was on the edge of sanity. His lower lip trembled as he tried to speak. "They told me they'd kill my family. I didn't want to do it... Please. I just want to go home."

His voice trailed off into gulping sobs, and his head dropped to his chest.

"You think this is some innocent young kid, Joe? You think we should treat him nice and get him back home safe?" He reached deep into the pocket of his robe. "You think we should feel bad for him because he misses his momma?" He pulled his hand from his pocket, and both Joe and Shepherd took a quick step back when they saw he'd withdrawn a pistol.

"Woah there, Arno," Joe said, trying to keep his voice calm and level. "Let's put the gun down, OK?

The kid ain't going anywhere. We can talk about this."

In the tense silence that followed Shepherd heard a quiet trickle, and he looked down to see liquid pooling at the feet of the prisoner. It ran down his leg, sluicing away the dried blood beneath his bandage before reaching the ground. Shepherd didn't know if it was the kid wetting himself or the American accent, but he couldn't help but feel pity for him despite everything. He didn't seem like a ruthless invading soldier. He was just a boy, shit scared and far from home.

"Come on, Novak, put it away," Shepherd pleaded. "We're not gonna let him go, but we don't want to execute a prisoner of war. We're better than that, right?"

Novak's knuckles were white as he tightly gripped the pistol, holding it firmly against his leg as if he was fighting himself for control of his gun hand. For a long moment it looked like he could go either way. The shed was frozen in a macabre tableau. Joe and Shepherd didn't dare move a muscle. Shepherd didn't even dare take a breath as Novak wrestled with the urge to fire.

The prisoner sat hunched over, his hands balled into fists and his teeth clenched, silently weeping as he waited for the shot. But it didn't come. Novak's better angels won whatever battle was raging within him, and his shoulders began to slump as his grip on the gun loosened. Shepherd slowly, quietly let out the breath he'd been holding, afraid that to make a sound might break the spell.

And then the kid broke it himself. He let out a gulping sob, turned to Novak and met his gaze with his one open eye. "I'm so sorry," he whispered, his voice quavering. "They made me do it."

The shot came too quickly for Shepherd to do anything, even if there was anything he *could* do. Even the kid barely had the time to let out a terrified yell.

Shepherd took a step back, shocked by the shot, his ears ringing with the deafening blast in the confined space. He stumbled against the rear wall of the shed, gripping a loose board with his fingers until his hearing began to return. When he finally looked up he saw Novak standing over the body, his shoulders slumped and the gun hanging loose at his side.

"Arno," Shepherd said, his own voice almost silent in his ears. "Arno, what have you done?"

Novak turned to Shepherd with tears in his eyes. He looked down at his hands, spattered with blood, and cocked the hammer on the pistol. "I couldn't let him... I..." He trailed off, shaking his head.

"Arno," Joe's voice was steady, authoritative but calm. "Put the gun down, Arno. It's all over now. It's OK. Nobody's going to jail here. You can relax."

Novak continued to shake his head, staring at his own bloodied hands, and in a quiet voice he spoke. "What he did to the Anderson girl..." He looked up at Joe, his voice suddenly angry. "Five years old. She was only five years old. You don't know. You didn't see it happen."

"Arno, please," Joe was a little more panicked now. It was clear he didn't have control of the situation, and neither did Shepherd. They were both caught up in the current, swept along with Novak's misery, anger and shame.

The old man's hands were shaking, and his voice came out in a whisper. "I never took a life. Seventy years and I never took a life. I'm sorry, Joe."

Joe took a slow step forward, approaching just as he would a wild animal. "It's OK, Arno, it's OK. You don't have to—"

"I didn't want it to be like this. Oh, God forgive me." Before Joe could take another step Novak brought the pistol up beneath his own chin.

Shepherd closed his eyes as the old man squeezed the trigger.

•▼•

:::**14**:::

COLE AND ABI waited patiently in the shade of the trees, nervously casting their eyes from the sunlight dappling the forest floor to the house half hidden in the trees. Abi felt naked without Shepherd's Glock, a gun she'd almost adopted as her own over the last twenty four hours, and she wished the guys would return soon with good news. This Novak guy seemed a little unhinged to her, and the sooner they could get away from his house the better.

She was finishing a cigarette when the gunshot rang through the trees, sending a flock of birds flapping into the air. She jumped at the sound, and after just a few seconds she realized that the shot could only have come from Novak himself. Neither Shepherd nor Big Joe had taken a weapon.

Cole hunkered down behind the gatepost, his eyes wide with fear, as Abi lowered herself flat on the ground and scanned the trees in the direction of the house.

"What do we do?" she hissed, desperate to tamp down the panic that had instantly sent her heart rate to a mile a minute.

Cole shrugged. "Did they leave the truck unlocked?"

"You want to run?" Abi couldn't quite believe his first impulse would be to abandon Joe and Shepherd and flee.

He shook his head. "No, I mean we should go get some guns! I left Shepherd's rifle on the back seat, and I'm guessing you have one back there. You think we can get to them?"

Abi searched through her memory. She couldn't remember seeing Shepherd lock the truck as they left it. The Jeep damned sure didn't have remote central locking, and she was sure she remembered closing her door after Shepherd had already started to walk away.

"Yeah, I think it's open. You know the way back through the thorns?"

Cole nodded, shooting a glance back towards the house before scurrying to the edge of the thick undergrowth, searching for the narrow gap where they'd broken through. "Here it is. Come on, follow me."

Abi hesitated for a moment, certain that another shot would come at any moment, this time in their direction, and then she steeled herself, took a deep breath and ran for the cover of the thorn bushes, following Cole into the thick foliage.

It took much longer to return to the road than it

had in the other direction, and by the time they finally got there Abi's legs were cut to ribbons by the spiky hedges. She ran to the truck, yanked open the rear passenger door and grabbed the Glock. Cole took the Ruger, looking ill at ease as he pulled it from the truck, holding it awkwardly like it was some kind of alien technology.

"You know how to use that?" she asked.

Cole shrugged. "Never fired a gun in my life. It's... ummm... you just point and shoot, right?"

Abi sighed inwardly. She didn't have time to teach a novice the basics. "Give it here." She took it from him, ejected and checked the magazine, clipped it back into place and drew back the bolt before passing it back to him, carefully. "*Now* you point and shoot. Keep your finger off the trigger. Don't get any crap in the barrel." She quickly moved to the side as Cole lifted the rifle to his shoulder. "And for God's sake, don't point it at anything you don't intend to kill. Especially me."

Cole blushed with embarrassment. "Sorry."

"It's OK. You have ten rounds in the magazine. You don't have to do anything but squeeze the trigger and the next round will load by itself. Now listen to me." She waited until she had his full attention. "Don't fire a single shot unless you know exactly what's going on. I don't want us accidentally starting our own little war thanks to a misunderstanding and an itchy trigger finger. Understand?"

Cole nodded. "Got it. Umm, maybe I should let you go ahead. You seem to know what you're doing."

"OK. Let's go." Abi turned to walk back to the gap in the bushes, the comforting weight of the Glock in her hand settling her nerves a little. She didn't have the heart to tell Cole that she was just as terrified as he was, but the fact that he thought she was some kind of expert markswoman just because she knew how to load a rifle gave her a measure of confidence she sorely needed.

Again it took several minutes to fight their way back through the thorns before the gate came into view. Abi wished she was wearing thicker trousers. The sharp barbs poked right through her thin sweatpants, and she could already see spots of blood blooming on the gray material as she scurried back to the gatepost, keeping low and out of sight. She reached an arm over the top and flipped the latch, carefully pushing the gate open as quietly as possible.

"Stay low, and keep behind me," she told Cole. "Keep the rifle against your chest as you move, and don't touch the trigger until you're ready."

He nodded nervously, and she turned back to the driveway and quickly worked her way along its edge, keeping to the bushes out of sight of the house. Suddenly she dropped to one knee and held a hand out behind her.

"Movement!" she hissed. Up ahead she saw figures shifting between the trees. More than one, she thought, but she couldn't be certain. The foliage was just too thick. She took a few steps forward, careful to avoid any twigs that might snap beneath her feet and reveal her position, trying to get a better view through the trees. She—

Suddenly a shot rang out. She fell to the ground and covered her head, but as the report echoed through the trees she realized it had come from behind her.

"Cease fire!" A voice called out from somewhere ahead, muffled and distant. "Abi! Is that you?"

She turned to face Cole and shot him a stern look, and Cole whispered "I'm sorry, I got scared."

"Yeah, it's me," she called back. "Are you OK?"

"Yeah. Don't shoot. Is it safe to come out?"

"Yeah, you're safe. Sorry, Cole has an itchy trigger finger."

Cole called out, his face pink with embarrassment. "Sorry, guys. My finger slipped."

Shepherd emerged warily from the trees a moment later, scowling at Cole. "I don't want to get shot with my own rifle, buddy," Shepherd chided. "Maybe hand it back to me?"

Cole stood and quickly gave up the gun with another apology, and Shepherd released the clip on the base of the barrel and split the rifle in two. "You know you should never put your finger on the trigger until you're ready to fire, right?"

"Tried to tell him," Abi said, flashing a quick grin in Cole's direction to let him know she wasn't mad. "No harm done. So how did it go? Is he gonna give us some guns?"

Shepherd hesitated before responding. "Ummm, yeah. Yeah, we're gonna get some guns, but first we have a few bodies to bury."

Abi and Cole followed Shepherd back to the shed as he explained what had happened, and while they were reluctant to waste their energy burying the Korean soldier and the crazy old man their attitude changed when Shepherd brought out the third body.

It was a little girl, her pink dress caked in dried mud and one of her blonde pigtails soaked red with blood. The bullet hole in her left temple was clearly visible, and Shepherd tactfully laid down the body in such a way that the exit wound wasn't.

"Novak was at the Anderson place just over the hill when they came," Shepherd explained. "I think he saw the soldier execute the girl."

"Oh, the poor thing." Abi had tears in her eyes as she took hold of a shovel and started digging. "How could anyone do that?"

Shepherd explained what he could piece together of the story as they dug. When he reached the part about the soldier's family back in North Korea he paused. "I don't know if it's true. Could be just something he said to try to stop Novak beating him."

Abi shook her head. "No, it's probably true. I've seen intel from our spy network in the country, such as it is, and it's a common tactic with the Koreans to use the threat of violence against family members to keep the people in line. One guy on his own might be willing to risk execution or the work camps for the chance to defect. If he succeeds he gets to live free, and if he fails he probably dies, but the important thing is that whatever happens he won't have to face a few more decades of hell. A personal deterrent isn't enough to stop him taking the risk, but if his family members are punished…"

She rested on her shovel and sighed. "The families of attempted defectors are usually exiled to the countryside. That's a nice way to say 'labor camps', by the way. If they're lucky they'll just be executed, but if not they'll be worked until they die of exhaustion. This is why only around thirty thousand people have successfully defected from the country over the years. Most of the folks who got out didn't have any family left back home. They didn't have to worry about what would happen to their mom and dad, their brothers and sisters, if they successfully made it over the border."

She looked down at the body of the soldier, and Shepherd could see there was a little pity in her eyes.

"I'm really no expert. I've only seen a few reports here and there, but if I had to guess I'd say that most of the Koreans over here aren't doing this because they hate us. Most of them are probably just following orders because the alternative is worse."

Shepherd frowned. He didn't know why, but it angered him to learn that this was all more complicated than he'd imagined. He wanted to see these soldiers as the embodiment of evil. He wanted to imagine them as zealots, crazed ideologues, completely devoted to their cause, if only because it would make it easier for him to pull the trigger when the time came.

"Sort of makes you not want to kill them, right?"

Abi nodded sadly. "I guess so." Her gaze drifted to the body of the little girl. "But we have to remember her when we squeeze the trigger. These kids may not be here of their own free will, but none of that matters. If they're willing to execute an innocent little girl they don't get any sympathy. I don't care how many people they have back home. There's a line, and they've crossed it."

A shrill whistle rang through the trees, and everyone stopped digging and turned in the direction of the house. "Shepherd," Joe called out. "I've found them. You wanna help with the heavy lifting?"

Shepherd buried his shovel in the ground and turned to Abi. "Do you mind?"

"No, go on, we can finish up here."

He smiled and turned towards the house, thankful to get away from the bodies and a little guilty about leaving the hard work to Abi and Cole, but they'd come here for a reason, and time wasn't on their side. The residents of Willow Falls were depending on them.

He found Big Joe waiting at the front door, and just as he was about to step onto the porch Joe waved his arms. "Woah, woah, woah, careful now. Novak sawed through a few of these boards." He pointed to a gap in the porch with the end of a cracked plank jutting up from the hole. "Crazy bastard booby trapped his own house. I'm pretty sure this one's safe." He tapped a toe on a plank running to the right of the door, and Shepherd carefully walked along it like a tightrope until he finally stepped inside.

"You find any traps in here?"

"Nothing yet. I don't think he was cuckoo enough to rig anything indoors, but... well, don't touch anything unless you absolutely have to. Now come on, they're in the back."

Shepherd followed Joe through the kitchen, watching his surroundings like a hawk for anything that might suddenly jump out at him, but by the time he reached the door leading off the kitchen he was fairly sure Joe was right. The house seemed not only free of traps but also remarkably well decorated.

Much nicer than his own home, in fact, and for a moment – before he caught himself and realized the thought was in incredibly bad taste – he wondered about moving into the house himself if the situation improved. He pushed the thought aside, surprised at himself for his own insensitivity. Christ, he'd watched Novak kill himself not a half hour ago.

"You thinking about moving in?"

Shepherd was surprised by the question. Was there something something in his expression that gave him away? "No! No, I..."

"Don't sweat it, I was thinking the exact same thing. Have you seen the size of that fireplace?"

"I was thinking more about the kitchen. See the big range oven? All I have back home is a little stove and a microwave." He stopped himself, again realizing the ghoulish nature of the conversation. "Let's stop talking about this. Where are the guns?"

Joe smiled as he pushed open the heavy oak door at the back of the kitchen. "Open sesame."

Shepherd's jaw dropped as he saw the room beyond. "Oh. My. God. Is that—?"

"Yes, sir. Yes it is," Joe grinned, playing a torch across the walls. "I think we're ready to go to war."

•▼•

:::15:::

THE ATMOSPHERE BACK on the road above Willow Falls had grown tense in the hours before dawn.

Since the truck had first stopped, four of the survivors of the 737 had begun to act unusually. Two had flat out refused to leave the back of the truck, despite the fact that the steel floor was sticky with Evan's blood and the sharp coppery odor pervaded the warm air. Rather than climb down and enjoy the fresh air the two had pinned down the canvas cover and almost immediately fallen asleep in the comforting darkness.

The third, a pale young woman, had fallen to her knees in the long grass at the side of the road and had spent the last two hours staring silently into the middle distance. The chief had tried to drum up conversation with her twice in an attempt to take her mind off things, but both times he'd been met by a brick wall of silence. It wasn't even clear that the woman could speak English.

The behavior of the three was a little worrying, but it was the final guy, Hal, who was keeping the chief's heart rate up. Hal was a large man who had a couple of inches and maybe thirty pounds on the chief, and since the truck had pulled to a halt he'd become increasingly agitated. He'd refused to help Samantha and the chief bury Evan, and after the others had left to find Novak he'd only become more of a worry. He paced back and forth like a caged animal, biting his fingernails down to the quick and checking his watch compulsively. Samantha could see blood at the edges of his nails, but the man didn't seem able to stop chewing on them.

The chief thought he knew what was happening, and it wasn't good. "They're all suffering psychological shock," he said, resting on the tailgate of Joe's truck and nursing a small bottle of water. "I've seen it a few times before, usually after bad car wrecks. Their minds don't know how to process what's happened. I mean, jeez, everything you guys have been through? A plane crash, a kidnapping and being forced to watch executions all in one day, on top of the fact that we've been invaded and hit by a damned EMP. I've only been through half of what you guys have suffered, and even I don't know how I'm still standing."

Samantha took a sip from her own water bottle. "So how come I'm... well, not quite OK, but how am I still thinking straight? I am thinking straight, aren't I? How would I know?"

"Don't worry, you seem OK to me." The chief nodded to the grave by the side of the road. He'd lashed together two sticks with his belt to form a cross, and Samantha had wrapped the epaulettes from Evan's captain's shirt to the horizontal. "You had something to occupy your mind. I don't want to make light of it, but digging that grave gave you the chance to take control of your situation. It let you feel like you were doing something productive, handling it rather than... I don't know, at its mercy. And besides, you're a stewardess. I'm sure you guys are trained to keep your head when everything's going to hell."

He fell silent for a moment, deep in thought. "Same with me, I suppose, and Big Joe, Shep and your pilot friend. We all have jobs that demand that we take charge and perform under pressure, even when we're scared out of our minds. But these guys..." His voice tailed off, and he gestured towards the truck.

"Who knows? Maybe they've never been tested with... ha, I was gonna say something like this. As if any of us have ever been through something this crazy. What I mean to say is maybe they've never been put under this kind of stress before. Y'know, watching as everything they thought was permanent – fixed forever, the foundations of our lives – comes crashing down?" He finished his water and moved to pull a cigarette from his pack. "Hell, I don't know. I'm no shrink. Maybe they're acting exactly as they should. Maybe *we're* the weird ones."

Over by the grass the catatonic woman began to move for the first time in an hour, lifting her knees up to her chest and rocking back and forth, still staring out to the middle distance. The chief sighed, grabbing a water bottle from the back of the truck. "I guess we're babysitting, in any case. Better go see if there's anything she needs."

He stepped away from the truck towards the young woman, and when he'd climbed over the steel crash barrier he dropped down to his haunches beside her, holding out the water bottle. "Thirsty?"

She didn't answer. Didn't even look in his direction. It was as if she was in a different world, trapped on the other side of a pane of one way glass, unable to even see the chief. She just rocked back and forth, her fingers clasped so tight around her knees her knuckles were white.

"I'll just leave this here for you, OK?" He set the bottle down beside her. "If you need anything to eat, or... well, if you need anything at all we're right over there by the truck. Just say the word." He waited an awkward moment, carefully studying her face for any signs of a reaction, but her expression could have been chiseled from stone. "OK, I'll just—"

A startled yell from behind him sent the chief spinning around on his heels, throwing himself off balance, and as he pushed himself to his feet and saw beyond the crash barrier his breath caught in his throat.

Hal was standing at the back of Joe's truck, and he'd grabbed the rifle the chief had found. Beside him Samantha had bolted to cover, hiding by the side of the truck, but there was nowhere for her to run. If Hal took it in his head to start firing she wouldn't stand a chance.

"Woah there, Hal," the chief said, holding up his hands. "Why don't you go ahead and set that gun down?" The fingers of his right hand twitched, an unconscious reflex as he prepared to reach for his own pistol, but he knew he wasn't wearing his holster. The soldiers had taken it from him when he'd been captured.

"I gotta get out of here," Hal said, gripping the rifle tight as he paced back and forth at the back of the truck. "Give me the keys to the truck," he demanded.

The chief nodded. "OK, Hal, that's no problem. No problem at all, buddy. You don't have to stay here if you don't want to. You can take the truck and just drive away, OK? Just let's get the others out from the back before you go. Deal?"

Hal hesitated for a moment, then nodded. "Don't try to play me, cop. Just toss the keys and get 'em out. I don't want to hurt anybody, but I will if I have to."

"I understand, Hal. You got nothing to worry about. I'm gonna get the keys, OK?" He slowly reached a hand to his pocket, picking out the keys with exaggerated movements. "I'm throwing them over to you." He took a single step forward and tossed the keys in a slow underarm arc, and Hal stepped forward to catch them.

The chief caught a movement in the corner of his eye. "No!" He barely had time to get out the word, but it was already too late. Samantha had bolted from the cover of the truck and launched herself towards Hal as he was distracted. She threw herself into a low tackle, catching him at his waist, but it was obvious it wouldn't be enough. Hal massively outweighed the flight attendant, and the tackle served only to throw him a little off balance. He caught the keys and swung the rifle around, and the chief responded with reflexes that hadn't been so sharp in a decade. He threw himself to the ground just as Hal squeezed the trigger, and he rolled away from the road as fully automatic fire peppered the steel crash barrier above him.

Again he found himself reaching for his absent pistol as the gunfire stopped, and he cursed as he lifted himself from the ground to see that Hal was already at the door of the troop truck, yanking it open and climbing in. By the time the chief vaulted the crash barrier the engine had already started, and as he tried to run towards the back – hoping to free the two passengers who didn't even know they were being abducted – the truck began to pull away, quickly outpacing the out of shape chief.

He stopped in the middle of the road, watching helplessly as the canvas cover at the back of the truck was raised. A woman's head poked out, her expression confused, but even if she wanted to jump down the truck was already moving too quickly. She gave a sad, confused wave to the chief as the truck reached the next turn in the road, and then she was gone.

The rumble of the engine faded once the truck was out of sight, and the chief cursed and ran his hands through his hair as he turned back to Joe's truck. He couldn't believe that had really happened. As if they didn't have enough shit to worry about, now they had Americans turning on each other.

"Samantha?" he called out. There was no response. "It's OK, he's gone. Where are you?"

His walk became a jog, which quickly became a sprint as the silence continued. By the time he reached Joe's truck his heart was pounding in his chest, but as he saw the streak of blood on the asphalt the pounding stopped. The world seemed to fall into slow motion as he saw a pair of feet poking out from behind the rear wheel, not moving.

"Samantha?" He already knew he wouldn't get an

answer as soon as he saw the feet, and as the body came into view all doubt was vanquished.

She'd taken a round in the neck, and another full in the chest. Even as the chief watched the pool of blood surrounding her grew wider. Her left hand was slick with blood where she'd pressed against the wound, but it seemed clear the bullet had severed her carotid. The blood seeped from the wound in a continuous stream. It was obvious her heart wasn't beating.

The chief rushed to the crash barrier as the vomit climbed to his throat. He doubled over and puked on the grass, his ears ringing and colored spots flashing before his eyes. None of this seemed real. He was certain he was going crazy, suffering from shock. He was sure that the moment he stood up and turned around he'd see Samantha sitting on the tailgate of Joe's truck smoking a cigarette, but as he looked down at his feet and saw the blood reach his boots he realized it was just a pipe dream. He wasn't crazy. He wasn't hallucinating. This was all horribly, painfully real.

He spat the last of the puke from his lips, wiping his mouth with the back of his hand as he stood, and that's when he realized he'd missed something. A laugh bubbled up from his stomach, a noise that came out of nowhere, completely uncontrolled and entirely unwanted. Once he started he couldn't stop. The laughter just kept coming. He kept laughing even as he fell to the ground at the edge of the pool of Samantha's blood. He kept laughing even as the laughter was joined by tears. Even as he felt the harsh, acid vomit burn his throat once again. Even as he looked back across the crash barrier, just to check that he wasn't imagining what he'd seen.

In the grass the catatonic young woman lay on her side, as if resting for a moment. Her knees were pulled up to her chest, and her hands rested loosely against them as if she'd drifted off to sleep. The chief couldn't see much blood, not from where he was standing. All he could see was the neat little hole punched into her temple where a stray round had caught her.

He realized he didn't even know her name. Nobody did. Even if anyone survived this, if they somehow came out on top and won their country back, nobody would ever know what had happened to this young woman. Her family would never know where she'd died, or how, or even where she was buried. Nobody would be left to set flowers on her grave

The chief pulled himself to his feet, climbed over the barrier and picked up the shovel Samantha had used to dig Evan's grave. He dug until the handle broke, and then he fell to his knees and continued to dig with the blade, and then with his fingers. And still he laughed, even as his fingers began to bleed. He laughed until it hurt, but even as the tears streamed down his face he couldn't stop.

•⸙•

:::16:::

IT TOOK SIX trips back and forth to clear out Novak's armory, and by the time the last gun was loaded the Jeep's suspension was visibly sagging at the rear.

"Are you sure we really need all of these guns?" Abi asked, pinned to the rear seat by the weight of an enormous ammo bag. "There's only a few of us, after all. What the heck are we gonna do with them?"

Big Joe nodded in the direction of Willow Falls. "There are around eight hundred people living down there, and less than half of them have guns. I want every adult in town armed to the teeth. And every kid, for that matter, as long as they can tell me which is the dangerous end by the second attempt."

Cole sat awkwardly beside Abi, his head mushed up against the window and the weight of a long wooden crate pressing down on his shoulder. "And what's this... thing I've got crushing me?"

Joe turned in his seat and grinned. "That, my friend, is a loaded and unused, A1, mint condition M72 light anti-tank weapon."

Cole shrugged. "I've no idea what that means."

"It means, Mr. Cole, that you have an incredibly illegal but incredibly I-don't-give-a-damn rocket launcher resting on your shoulder." He grinned maniacally, his eyes bright with excitement. "We're going to go down there and show those bastards what happens when you try to mess with Virginia. I'll give you a hint. Things explode."

Cole froze in his seat, his eyes wide. "You're telling me I have a rocket launcher a few inches from my face? And you didn't think you should warn me?"

Joe shook his head. "Well, I figured you were due a little payback for shooting at Shep. Might not be the worst thing in the world if you got blown up, know what I'm saying?"

Shepherd glanced in the rear view, breaking into a smile as he saw that Cole was holding his breath, eyes closed and face pale. "Don't worry, he's just screwing with you. Those things are completely harmless until you extend the launcher and activate the firing mechanism. You could juggle the damned things and nothing would happen." He looked back at the mirror and saw that Cole wasn't convinced. "No, seriously. A friend of mine once had a misfire with one of them at a shooting range somewhere in Asia. He froze up and waited for it to explode in his hands, but the guy who ran the place just walked over with a cigarette hanging from his lips, gave it a good smack and handed it back. It fired the second time. Don't sweat it, they're as safe as a house brick until they're primed."

"OK…" Cole didn't sound entirely convinced, but he seemed to relax a little from his terrified rictus. "And why exactly do we need a rocket launcher when we have all these guns?"

"Because," Shepherd explained, "they have at least one Humvee still rolling, or two if your stunt with the fireworks didn't burn out the other. Novak's biggest, baddest bullets are .308 Winchesters, and if those Humvees have any armor at all we'll have a hell of a time piercing it with hunting rifles. That bad boy resting ever so lightly on your shoulder will cut through eight inches of steel plate like a hot knife through butter."

Big Joe spoke up. "Yeah, and if you think we'd leave behind something like that for the sake of…" His voice trailed off as he saw what was up ahead. "What the hell?"

Shepherd slowed as he noticed what was wrong. Up ahead Joe's truck was sitting where they'd left it at the side of the road, but the troop truck was nowhere to be seen. More worryingly, none of the six people they'd left behind were there, even though they must have heard the approaching engine.

"You think we should pull up short?" Shepherd asked, already pulling to the side of the road.

"Uh huh," Joe agreed, opening the glove box and

pulling out his Sig. "Guys, grab a weapon and get ready to take cover."

Shepherd picked up his Mossberg from between the seats as he pulled in at an angle, presenting the Jeep broadside to Joe's truck about twenty yards away. He pointed to Joe's door, and after Joe climbed out Shepherd awkwardly followed. Cole and Abi somehow managed to extricate themselves from the weaponry in the back and finally joined them.

"You guys wait here," Shepherd whispered. "Joe, you mind covering me?" He crept to the back edge of the Jeep and peered out, steeling himself for the break across open ground, and then scurried quickly to the steel crash barrier at the side of the road, his Mossberg braced against his chest. When he reached the barrier he rolled under it, coming to rest in the tall grass with the shotgun pointed straight ahead.

There was a noise coming from up ahead, a kind of soft mewling, like an injured animal. Shepherd cautiously lifted himself to his knees, and through the grass he saw...

"Chief?" He got no response, and called louder. "Chief, is that you?"

Up ahead the figure finally seemed to respond. Shepherd climbed to his feet, fully exposed but almost certain he didn't have to worry about any attackers. Up ahead the chief was slumped on his knees, his shoulders heaving with gulping tears. His hands were caked in dirt, and as Shepherd slowly approached he saw there were now two bodies on the grass beside the road. The chief had been trying to dig graves with his hands.

"Chief, what the hell happened? Where is everyone?" He rushed closer now, grabbing the chief by his shoulder.

In two decades of knowing the man Shepherd had never once seen Chuck Roberts cry, not even the day he'd lost his wife to cancer. He'd always been stoical and steady, a rock of stability whatever was going on. Now, seeing the red rings around his eyes and the two clean lines on his cheeks where the tears had cut through the dirt, Shepherd felt completely untethered from anything he recognized as normality. To see this man broken, weeping...

The chief wiped his face and sniffed, looking up at Shepherd through bloodshot eyes, and he nodded towards the crash barrier. Beside it the two bodies were laid out straight, their arms folded across their chests.

"I... it was all my fault. I shouldn't have left the gun just sitting there. I should have known he'd go for it. Shouldn't have left a man in his condition alone."

Shepherd didn't know what he was talking about, but right now he could see it wasn't important. The chief just needed to talk. He needed to get the words out, to let out the shame and grief so he might, somehow, be able to keep going without it destroying him.

"Samantha was just trying to help. She was brave, Shep, real brave. Braver than I've ever been. She just wasn't strong enough to stop him, and..." He dropped his head, resting his hands on his knees as he took a deep, shuddering breath. Finally he looked up.

"Would you pray with me, Shep?"

•▼•

:::**17**:::

IN THE DARKNESS of the Willow Falls diner
Park Ju-Won sat on the floor against the back wall,
her fingernails digging so deep into her palms they
drew blood, but she barely noticed the pain. Right
now she only felt numb. None of this felt real.

She stared transfixed at the body at her feet, a
short, heavy set middle aged man in military fatigues,
four silver stars stitched to the red and gold insignia
on his shoulders. She tried to drag her eyes away but
they kept returning to the prone body, blood
glistening in his matted hair. She could feel the panic
rising in her chest, and she tried to keep herself calm
by repeating the mnemonic for the bones of the skull
she'd had drummed into her through her years at
medical school. STEP OF SIX. Sphenoid. Temporal.
Ethmoid. Parietal. Occipital. Frontal... Sphenoid,
temporal, ethmoid... *Sphenoidtemporalethnoid...*

This was the first man she'd ever killed.

She hadn't planned to do it. Not consciously,
anyway. She'd only walked into the diner to escape
for a moment, to take a break from the insanity and
just sit by herself in the darkness until the world

came into focus once more. She'd had no idea that her *Daewi* – her Captain – was already inside, and when she'd seen what he was trying to do to the large woman who seemed to own the place...

It was just the last straw. The stress had been building up inside her for the last few days, ever since her handler had arrived to collect her from her dorm and bundle her off to her staging point in Richmond, and it had only grown worse after the madness of the last twenty four hours.

The only thing that had kept her from snapping was the thought that this would keep her family safe. She could just do her job and keep her head down, and in return her mother would be allowed to live in peace. Maybe she'd even be permitted to join her once the offensive was over and they'd secured their hold on the country. Ju-Won would go to the ends of the earth for the chance to see her mother again, and she'd do almost anything to keep her alive and safe.

Almost anything, but not *that*.

Ju-Won's fate was sealed the moment she walked into the diner and caught Jeong Hwan, her superior officer, trying to do *that* to a woman. Standing there with a pistol in hand and his pants around his ankles, the American woman cowering before him. Her mother would have never forgiven her if she knew the price of her freedom had been for Ju-Won to stand by and allow *that* to happen.

She'd barely thought about it before she did it. It was as if she was running on autopilot, operating on instinct and white hot rage alone. She'd raced across the room and grabbed the first thing to hand, a heavy steel bucket resting on the bar, filled with some kind of oil. She'd taken the handle in both hands and swung it with all her might. She'd felt it connect with Jeong Hwan's head. She'd watched as he fell to his knees, stunned, and she'd felt her arms draw back to deliver a second blow, this time pinning his skull between the bucket and the steel edge of a booth table. She'd probably imagined it, but she was almost sure she'd heard his skull crack.

A depressed fracture of the temporal bone. That's what had killed him. She could see the dent, the deep misshapen depression just above his right ear where the sharp corner of the table had been driven into his skull like a chisel. More than likely the fracture was comminuted, sending shards of bone into his brain, piercing the meninges and causing a massive hemorrhage. Almost certainly fatal without a skilled surgeon on hand. Even if Ju-Won had wanted to help him there was nothing she could have done. She didn't have nearly enough training to perform such a complex surgery, and her medical kit in the Humvee was only packed for standard battlefield injuries.

She barely remembered what had happened next. She was only dimly aware that the woman Jeong

Hwan had been assaulting had pulled herself from the ground and fled as Ju-Won fell to the ground and pummeled the body with her fists. She didn't even know how much time had passed. It felt like just moments since she'd killed him, but already the pre-dawn light in the windows grew brighter.

She knew she was running out of time. Soon enough the Humvee would be finished with its sweep of the western suburbs, and would return to take her back to the internment camp at the edge of town. She'd need to get her story straight, to explain that she'd walked into the diner and found *Daewi* Jeong already injured, attacked by one of the Americans. That she'd tried to save the *Daewi*, but his injuries had been just too severe.

But... but what if this led to reprisals against the Americans? By now they must have dozens of prisoners, if not hundreds, and if there's one thing she'd learned about *Chungjwa* Choi Jun-Ho, the Lieutenant Colonel, it's that he wouldn't hesitate for a moment before executing prisoners. He seemed to take a perverse pleasure in it, and Ju-Won knew the reason. He wasn't like the rest of them.

Many of the Koreans were, like Ju-Won, long term sleepers. Some of them had spent years in the United States, infiltrating the country at every level, laundering funds, preparing supplies, gathering intelligence and working to minimize the home team tactical advantage. Ju-Won herself had been in the country four years, in deep cover at a medical school in Ohio, and she suspected that many of the others had, like her, grown a little too fond of their adoptive home. She hadn't dared ask them outright, of course, but she suspected that many really didn't want to be here, leading an attack on the country that had introduced them to the wonders of the Avengers, NASCAR, the McDonalds Big Mac and the idea of freedom itself.

If the others were anything like her they were intoxicated by the United States, entranced by the freedom to do and say and eat and drink and watch and read and listen to whatever they damned well pleased. That was the power of the United States. It was like junk food: unhealthy and fattening, but deliciously addictive. After three years Ju-Won was hooked, hopelessly and completely in love with the country she'd been sent to help destroy.

The *Chungjwa* was different. Choi Jun-Ho was a true believer, flown in just a couple of days ahead of the EMP and untainted by the magical decadence of the States. He hadn't learned his English from Hollywood movies or in bars, flirting with cute college students, but in a grim concrete office block in Pyongyang. He'd never been exposed to the food, drink, TV, movies and music that had seeped into Ju-Won's soul and softened her resolve to serve her motherland. The *Chungjwa's* resolve was firm, and his purpose divine. He would not hesitate to kill ten thousand Americans if it helped him advance a single inch towards his goal.

Ju-Won felt the panic return. She was sure now that as soon as word got back to the *Chungjwa* the reprisals would begin. In saving the life and the honor of the woman in the diner she'd surely sacrificed many more. Her compatriots would carry Jeong Hwan's body back to the *Chungjwa's* feet, and in response he would use his pistol until he ran dry of ammunition.

… Unless they never found the body.

She pulled herself awkwardly to her feet, slipping in the layer of pungent cooking oil that had spilled from the bucket. There wasn't much blood. Apart from the oil on the floor there would be little evidence that anyone had ever been here. If she could only hide the body well enough perhaps the *Chungjwa* would believe Jeong Hwan had fled. Perhaps he'd still decide to execute the prisoners, but there was a chance the uncertainty would keep his finger from the trigger.

She grabbed the collar of Jeong Hwan's shirt in one hand and pulled, relieved that the oil on the ground helped lubricate the passage of her overweight superior, and dragged him around to the kitchen door. Somewhere in there must be a space large enough to hide him from view. A freezer, perhaps, or maybe even a dumpster out back. Once he was gone she could simply run a mop across the diner floor to obscure the drag marks, head out front and wait for the Humvee to collect her. There was no need for anyone to know she'd even seen him.

Once the trail of oil ran out the *Daewi* was much more difficult to drag. He outweighed Ju-Won by fifty pounds, and she quickly tired of bending at the waist and shuffling backwards. Halfway through the kitchen she took a break, sliding down the side of a fridge and shaking her hands to relieve her aching fingers. For a moment she closed her eyes, resting her head against the fridge and wishing she could grab just a few moments of sleep, her first in two days.

She saw the lights of the approaching Humvee glow red through her closed eyes, and as she opened them she saw the glow play through the serving window across the walls of the kitchen. She sprang to her feet as the light stopped moving, and ducked her head when she realized the vehicle had parked right out front of the diner.

With a sudden burst of energy she grabbed Jeong Hwan's collar and hauled him back at twice the speed, straining every muscle in her body to get him back to the walk in freezer at the far end of the kitchen. There were only a few yards left to go, and then she'd be able to step out the emergency exit at the back of the diner and work her way around to the square to meet the Humvee. She'd—

"Stop right there, missy, and tell me what in the holy Hell's going on or I swear to God I'll start shooting."

Ju-Won froze. The voice came from the shadows to her left, and as she slowly turned her head a figure stepped out into the glow of the headlights. It was her, the woman Jeong Hwan had been attacking. An overweight woman with a rosy complexion and a Stars and Stripes apron wrapped around her waist. In her hand was a pistol.

"Well? Do you speak English, or are we gonna talk in the universal language of ass kicking?"

Ju-Won nodded. She dropped Jeong-Hwan's collar and raised a finger to her lips as the front door of the diner creaked open. Korean voices. A laugh. A question. Another chuckle.

She raised both hands and took a slow, deliberate step towards the woman, all too aware of the gun leveled at her chest.

"Please be quiet," she whispered. "I'm not here to hurt you, but *they* are." She jabbed a finger towards the front of the diner. "Don't make a sound, and they should leave."

The woman narrowed her eyes, clearly unsure whether to trust Ju-Won, but after a moment she nodded. She even lowered the gun a little, but only to point it at Ju-Won's stomach rather than her chest. It wasn't much of an improvement.

For what felt like an eternity Ju-Won held her breath, waiting for the door to creak once more as the men left. From where she was standing she could only faintly hear their conversation. Both of them spoke Korean in the thick, lazy dialect of the north eastern rural provinces. They were looking for Jeong Hwan in the darkness, and they were confused.

"He said we should meet him here, right?" one asked.

"Yes. Is this the only restaurant? He said to meet him in the restaurant, but he didn't say which one. Maybe there's another?"

"Should we go look?"

She didn't hear a response, but she guessed it was a yes. She heard the wet, cautious slap of footsteps through the slippery oil, followed by a creak. Still she held her breath, and for a moment she heard nothing but her own heart pounding in her ears.

And then a voice. A question. A curse. An exclamation.

She closed her eyes, and her heart sank.

She looked down at Jeong Hwan's body resting at her feet. At the empty holster attached to his hip.

They'd found his gun.

•▾•

:::18:::

SHEPHERD SHOOK OUT the pain in his hands and looked down at his bruised and bloodied fingers.

He'd had just about enough of this. The sun was barely halfway up, and they were already on their sixth burial of the day. The pilot. Novak. The little Anderson girl and the Korean kid. By the time he'd finished digging Samantha's grave with the remains of the folding shovel he barely had enough energy left to dig another for...

Damn, he didn't even know her name. It hadn't occurred to him to ask. She was just some random woman, one of the survivors from Cole's plane crash. He hadn't even noticed her when she'd climbed down from the back of the truck. She was just a... a blank. Shepherd didn't want to think too hard about what it meant that, just a day after the power went out, burying the dead had already become a dull chore rather than a profound tragedy.

The hole was only just deep enough to hold the young woman by the time his reserves were completely drained. He wished he had more in him, enough to bury her with a little more dignity, and with more than a few inches of cover, but he'd done all he could. Any deeper and he'd have so little energy he'd probably end up in the ground himself.

"Shep?" Big Joe waved to attract his attention, beckoning him over to Joe's truck. He handed over a candy bar. "I think they'll need a few minutes." He nodded over to Cole and the chief, each of them lifting a body and slowly carrying them over to the graves. The chief was still a mess, his eyes bloodshot and his nose streaming, but Cole just seemed enraged. He carried himself as if every muscle was a bunched fist, and once he'd carefully lowered Samantha's body into the hole he scooped the soil back in as if it had talked about his mother.

"Might want to keep the rocket launcher away from him," Joe said, pointing to Cole. "I wouldn't put it past him to try to blow up the world right now."

Shepherd nodded. Nothing more dangerous than an angry guy with his finger on a trigger. "So, what's the game plan?"

"Chuck tells me they got some kinda makeshift prison out at the park ground. I'd guess that's where they're planning to gather folk, if they haven't already, so we gotta hit 'em hard right there. Go in quick from every angle, before they have a chance to think." He gestured towards the back of the truck. "I got Abi loading a bunch of Novak's rifles. If we get the chance we can hand them out along the way to anyone we can find. You'll be the point man on the M72, if you're okay with that. I'd love to do it myself, but the damned thing'd toss me back fifty yards the second I pulled the trigger."

"No, I'm happy to do it. It's about time we got some payback."

"Then the second you see that Humvee you let her rip. Far as I can tell that's their last vehicle. Once we take it out they'll have to use the civilian cars we got running, and the .308s won't have any trouble piercing them." He looked over Shepherd's shoulder. Cole and the chief were already returning from the graves. "Boys, we can sit a spell if you want to properly pay your respects."

The chief shook his head. "If it's OK with you, Joe, and I'm pretty sure it's OK with Cole, we just want to get down there and kill some folks, know what I mean?"

Joe looked unsure, but he settled as Shepherd gave him an almost imperceptible nod. "Well, if you think you're ready." He yelled out. "Abi? How you coming with those guns?"

"I'd say we're all set," she replied, scooping up a half dozen rifles in the crook of her arm. "You guys take these. Jim and I will take the rest." She walked slowly back to Joe's truck, struggling under the weight, and set the rifles down on the back seat before returning to Shepherd's truck and climbing into the driver's seat.

"Hey, who said you were driving?" Shepherd complained, heading for the driver's side.

Abi smiled as she turned the key. "Big Joe," she replied. "You can't exactly drive and fire this thing at the same time, right?" She pointed to the front passenger seat, where the M72 rested in the footwell beside Shep's Ruger. "Come on, don't get all butthurt. You get to play with your boy's toy."

Grudgingly Shepherd walked around to the passenger side. He'd never let anyone drive his truck before, but he figured that if there was ever a day for firsts then today was that day. He was about to drive into his home town and fire a rocker launcher at a Humvee full of North Korean invaders. It seemed a little childish to complain that he didn't get to do it from his favorite seat.

Abi threw the truck in gear, struggling for a moment with the busted gearbox, and turned it back in the direction of Willow Falls. Big Joe followed close after, and as they reached the foot of the hill he overtook the Jeep, taking point. From his place in the front passenger seat Shepherd could see the barrel of a rifle emerge through a window. Moments later the chief appeared through the sun roof, closely followed by a shotgun.

"So *that's* what he meant when he said he'd clear a path," Abi said. "I thought he meant... I don't know, that he'd make sure we didn't hit any roadblocks or something. Damn, that's brave of him to take the lead."

Shepherd remained silent, clutching the tube of the M72. He knew that Big Joe was the ballsiest sonofabitch in three counties, but it wasn't courage that had made him take the lead. Like Shepherd, Joe knew that the most important thing in either of the trucks wasn't any of the people. It was the rocket launcher. Everything – and every*one* – else was expendable, but as long as the Koreans had control of a Humvee they could run the town, especially if it was heavily armored. The M72 was the only weapon they had that had a chance of taking it out in one shot, and without it they'd have no choice but to put themselves in the line of fire and hope they could breach the bulletproof windows before the Koreans returned fire.

Up ahead Joe slowed his truck as he reached the edge of town. Here the occasional home gave way to the dense suburbs, and for a few moments Joe pulled to a stop with the engine idling, searching around for movement. Were people still in their homes, hiding from the sound of the engine, or had they all been taken?

Shepherd felt the launcher tube slip against his sweaty palms as he scanned the closest windows, searching for the slightest twitch of a curtain, or movement in the shadows.

Nothing. Apart from the rumble of their engines the suburbs were silent as the grave. Shepherd found himself whispering a prayer that his friends and neighbors were safe, but something told him many had not survived the night. There weren't enough hidey holes in town for eight hundred people to evade capture.

The chief waved from the sunroof as Joe moved on, and Abi crawled forward. She stared straight ahead and spoke in a low voice. "Just stay calm. We'll be fine. Don't lose it, OK."

Shepherd forced a smile. "I'm good, no need for a pep talk."

Abi shook her head. "I was talking to myself. I can hardly breathe, my heart's pounding so fast."

"Don't worry. Just hang back a little. If Joe hits any trouble we'll have plenty of warning." He tried to sound convincing, but if he was honest with himself he'd have to admit he was just as scared as Abi. For one thing, he'd never fired an M72, or any kind of rocket launcher. He'd stared at the firing instructions printed on the side of the outer tube until he could recite them by heart, but he knew he was so jittery there were even odds that when the time came he'd end up firing it backwards.

Up ahead Joe took a left onto Main Street, and Shepherd held his breath as the chief crouched down, scanning the road for signs of the enemy. Abi let out a nervous yelp as the chief suddenly leveled his shotgun at something, but a moment later he lowered it, turned back towards the Jeep and gave a thumbs up and an embarrassed grin.

"What the hell's he doing? The guy almost gave me a heart attack."

Shepherd pointed at the road up ahead. "There's your culprit." A brown spaniel trotted out into the street without a care in the world. As Joe's truck passed by it paused and yelped up at the chief, who looked down at it and smiled.

The shot came out of nowhere. Just a couple of seconds after the chief turned towards the dog he was knocked back against the edge of the sunroof as if from a heavy blow. He slumped forward at the waist, and through the rear windshield Shepherd saw Cole drag him back into the car as Joe planted his foot on the gas.

Shepherd didn't even see the shooter, but Joe sure did. Just a moment after the chief fell back into the truck it veered to the left and slammed into a Hyundai parked by the side of the road. Joe threw the truck into reverse, pulled back a few yards and then jumped out, drawing his Sig as he climbed down.

There was no need for him to fire. By the time Abi and Shepherd caught up it was clear what had happened. Joe had caught a young man in fatigues between his truck and the Hyundai, crushing the life out of him in an instant. The poor bastard hadn't even had the time to get off a second shot.

Shepherd jumped out of the Jeep and ran to the back of Joe's truck, yanking open the rear door. "Chief? You OK?"

The chief nodded, lying awkwardly on the back seat and clutching his right arm. "Yeah," he said, sounding more annoyed than in pain. "He just winged me. Barely broke the skin." He pulled his hand away, and Shepherd was relieved to see that there was very little blood. "Thank God that dog distracted me," he said, pulling himself upright. "I think I've got my very own guardian angel looking out for me."

Joe climbed back up to the driver's seat, holstering his pistol. "I hope we've all got one, Chuck. I don't want to see any more bodies today. How you holding up?"

"Good to go." The chief looked pale and shaken, but he made an effort to play it off as nothing. "Just point me in the right direction and I'll start shooting."

"Maybe stay in the truck from now on, Chief, y'hear?" Shepherd pushed closed the door and leaned in the open window. "You're too big a target to stand up there."

The chief let out a strained laugh. "The diet starts tomorrow. Now go on, get outta here. The longer we stay out here yapping the more people'll take potshots at my fat ass."

Shepherd nodded and returned to the Jeep, climbing in as Abi gunned the engine. If anything he felt even more nervous now than he had before. Enemies could be waiting behind every car. They could be sighting Shepherd through a scope from the darkness of a distant window. At any moment his world could erupt in gunfire, and the thought of that only made the powerless silence of the town all the more oppressive.

Joe pulled away, a little more cautiously now, and through the rear windshield Shepherd could see that everyone in the truck ahead was crouching just a little lower. So were Shepherd and Abi, now he thought to notice. Shepherd's view of the road ahead was cut off by the hood of the car as he slumped low in the chair, and he only hid lower as they approached the end of Main Street and headed towards the small town square. From here it would only be a short ride out through the wealthy suburbs to the park ground, and only God knew what would be waiting for them out there.

Shepherd watched as Big Joe pulled into the square, and frowned curiously as the brake lights lit up at the back of the truck. It pulled to a stop, and a moment later he felt his muscles tense and bunch as the engine cut out and Cole waved frantically out the rear window. He jabbed a finger towards something unseen in the square, over in the direction of Pam's diner, and in the air he traced the shape of a vehicle.

"Do you think he means..." Abi pulled the Jeep to a halt. "Oh God, is it the Humvee?"

Shepherd grabbed the tube of the rocket launcher and raised it to the window. As soon as Cole saw it he nodded, still pointing towards the square, and without a word Shepherd pushed open his door and climbed out of the truck, leaving it open so as not to make any more sound than absolutely necessary.

The town square fell silent as Abi killed the Jeep's engine. There was absolutely no sound but for Shepherd's own pulse beating so loud he was sure it could be heard a mile away. From where he stood he could see nothing but Joe's truck and the remains of the fire the townsfolk had built by the willow tree, and it was with a surreal, otherworldly feeling that he made his way towards the corner of the general store at the edge of the square.

Not twelve hours ago hundreds of revelers had stood before the fire enjoying burgers and the company of their friends. They'd agreed to face whatever the future brought together, as a family, but none of them had expected that the future might hold Humvees driven by the soldiers of an invading army.

Shepherd reached the corner and dropped to one knee as he spotted the vehicle. It was parked haphazardly out front of Pam's diner, halfway onto the sidewalk with both front doors wide open. A sitting duck, and an easy target even for someone who'd never used a rocket launcher before.

Shepherd released the catch on the launcher and pulled it to its full length, hearing the dull metallic click as the mechanism inside the tube armed the rocket. He clicked the front sight into place, hefted the heavy tube to his shoulder and took a deep, slow breath as he centered the Humvee in the sight.

This would be easier than he thought. No returning fire. Not even any soldiers present as he squeezed the trigger and destroyed their fire superiority in one fell swoop. This would be a piece of cake.

He turned back towards Big Joe's truck for a final check, just to make sure they had his back, then returned to the sight and took a final breath. His finger closed over the trigger mechanism, a soft pad that needed to be gently squeezed to release the rocket, and he felt the resistance beneath his fingers. One. Two. Thr—

His fingers twitched as he spotted movement behind the Humvee. It wasn't much, just a shifting shadow on the ground behind the truck, but he didn't want to take any chances that it was a friendly. He lifted his fingers from the trigger and took another breath, blinking the sweat from his eyes.

Ten seconds. That's all he'd give them. If the person behind the truck didn't leave in the time it took him to draw three deep breaths he'd fire anyway. He couldn't risk calling out to warn them, but he didn't want to —

A figure emerged, and Shepherd returned his hand to the trigger.

It was a Korean. A young woman, dressed in military fatigues and carrying a bag at her waist.

She deserved no warning, and she wouldn't get one.

Shepherd felt his heart pound in his throat as he closed his fingers over the trigger and squeezed. Time seemed to slow. Beneath his grip he felt the firing mechanism kick into action. The pent up energy of the rocket bunched like a coiled spring, ready to burst from the tube as soon as the accelerant began to burn.

And then he saw her.

It was Pam, emerging from the diner and taking the bag from the Korean woman. She was still wearing the Stars and Stripes apron she'd worn the night before, but now it was stained with blood. In the split second after Shepherd squeezed the trigger he took in every detail. She stood casually, relaxed in the presence of the Korean. There was a smile on her face. She didn't look as if she was a prisoner, or that she was doing anything under duress. She looked... she looked like they were friends.

All of this took just a fraction of a second to process, but it was more than enough time for Shepherd to make a decision. In the instant the rocket burst into life he leaned back, falling against the wall of the convenience store as the front of the tube cracked open and the tip of the rocket emerged. It was hardly any movement at all, but it was enough to throw off his aim. The rocket burst out into the air, screaming forward with a trail of bright smoke emerging from its rear, and Shepherd held his breath until he saw that it cleared the Humvee by just a few inches and screamed into the side wall of the town hall.

All hell broke loose. Pam and the Korean threw themselves to the ground as the wall exploded, throwing shrapnel far across the square. Shepherd dropped the spent rocket tube as it began to sear his shoulder. Behind him he heard Big Joe climb from his truck and start yelling, but for the life of him he couldn't make out a word as Joe started to fire.

The gunfire continued for what felt like an eternity, Joe's gun joined by Cole's, Abi's and the chief's. Nobody seemed to know what they were firing on, but the Humvee seemed like the favorite target. It took a while for Shepherd to realize that the other's hadn't seen what he'd seen. They hadn't noticed Pam, or the Korean woman. They must have assumed that Shepherd had missed accidentally, and they were now trying to finish the job without his help.

"Cease fire!" he yelled, his voice drowned out by the gunfire. He waved his arms and the air and stood up straight, risking placing himself in the line of fire. "Joe, for the love of God stop shooting!"

One by one the guns fell silent, his friends holding back if only out of confusion, and when Cole finally took his finger from the trigger silence once again descended on the square.

"Thank you!" Shepherd yelled, his own voice muffled and quiet in his damaged ears. He turned back to the Humvee. "Pam! Are you OK?"

Behind him he heard confused conversation, and a bemused yell as Pam finally emerged from the door of the diner waving a white dishtowel in the air. "If this is how you guys treat your friends I don't wanna be your enemy."

Shepherd broke into a jog, closing the distance between him and the diner in a few seconds, and he peered through the door in search of the Korean woman. Part of his confused mind thought he might have imagined her, but that part was silenced when he saw the young woman poke a fearful head above the counter.

"Ummm... what's going on?" He couldn't think of anything else to say.

Pam took a step forward, standing between Shepherd and the Korean woman. "I'll tell you, but you gotta get your guys to stand down first. They're not gonna like what they see. Agreed?"

Shepherd nodded. "Agreed. Are you OK?"

Pam nodded. "I'm better than OK. I've got myself a Humvee, a buddy and a couple of prisoners, if you can resist the urge to blow any of them up."

"You have prisoners?" He frowned, baffled beyond belief. The Korean woman didn't look like she was a prisoner.

Pam pulled the door wide and beckoned Shepherd through. "You'd better come in. This is all getting a little complicated."

•▼•

:::19:::

IT TOOK TEN minutes to convince Big Joe to holster his Sig Sauer before entering the diner. After he'd learned who was in there he was ready to go in guns blazing, and Cole and the chief weren't far behind him.

Eventually it was Pam who brought him back down to earth. Besides Big Joe she was the bedrock of Willow Falls, a woman who'd been a fixture in the town's diner ever since she'd been a little girl. Joe didn't like it one bit, but he knew that if Pam vouched for the person inside he could take her at her word. The Korean woman was off limits. She was to be treated as a non-combatant, and if anyone had a problem with that they'd have to take on Pam herself, and the shotgun she held at her belly like a protective amulet.

The other two Koreans, on the other hand...

"So what are you saying?" Big Joe asked. "Are you telling me she mutinied against her own army?"

Pam nodded. "She's a good girl, Joe. She saved my life, for one thing, and I don't think she wants to be here any more than you or me."

Joe and Shepherd exchanged glances. They'd already heard this story once before, from Novak's prisoner, and they knew it didn't hold any water if the girl had taken any lives. Shepherd told Pam the story, and she angrily shook her head.

"She ain't killed a soul, I swear to you. Well, aside from her own commander, but like I said she had a good reason for that. If it hadn't been for her God knows what would have happened to me."

"I'm a medic." The voice took Shepherd by surprise. These were the first words he'd heard from the Korean, and he wasn't expecting them to sound so... American. She sounded almost native born, with barely a trace of an accent. "I was sent here to study medicine. I'm not a soldier. I've never even fired a gun. That was..." She nodded towards the far wall of the diner, where two bloodied figures lay hogtied on the ground. "That was their job." She spat the words angrily, and Shepherd had no doubt that her distaste was genuine.

"And I suppose you've got family back home in Korea with guns pointed at their heads?" Again, Shepherd had heard this story before.

"We all have. My mother is in Pyongyang. Or at least that's where she was when I left the country. I don't know if she's still alive." The sadness in her voice stabbed at Shepherd's heart. "It's how they control us. It's how they've built an army willing to risk everything to invade. Do you think any of us really want to be here? Do you think we're monsters? Do you think we wouldn't rather stay at home and live in peace?"

Cole stepped forward, his fists clenched. "I watched one of your men execute three of ours in cold blood. I watched him shoot them dead without blinking. Does he just want to live in peace?"

The woman shook her head. "The *Chungjwa*. He's our commander. And no, he doesn't want peace. We're not... we're not all good people."

"But you are?"

"I'm... I don't know. I don't think it's as simple as good and bad. I just know I don't want to do this any more. I want to keep my mother safe, but I know she'd rather die than live with a daughter who helped people kill to save her. She... she just wanted me to be a doctor. She wanted me to help people, and I've betrayed her."

"And you think we're just going to—"

"Stop, please. I don't think anything. I don't expect your forgiveness, and I don't deserve it. I just want to help you. I want to help make this right."

Cole bristled with anger. "If you want to help us you should take a gun and put a bullet in your brain."

"Cole!" Big Joe took a step forward, placing himself between Cole and the woman.

"You'll keep a civil tongue, son, or you'll have me

to answer to." Pam drew herself up to her full height and stared down the pilot.

Cole was undeterred. "In fact, why don't we get rid of these two while we're here?" He stepped away from Joe towards the two prisoners, grabbing his rifle from a table as he walked. "Way I see it, the only good Korean is a dead Korean."

He didn't see the blow coming. Before he'd taken his second step Pam raised her shotgun and thrust the butt into the back of his head, sending him tumbling to the ground. He fell face first into a table and bounced like a coconut from the surface, his legs collapsing like jelly as he fell.

"That's the last we'll hear of that," Pam said, resting the shotgun on her shoulder. "We had a hell of a time tying those bastards up without killing them, and I'm not gonna see my hard work go to waste. You people understand me? There'll be no more killing in my diner."

A stunned silence fell over the room. Cole clutched his head on the floor as Pam kicked his rifle away, and Shepherd pushed his own Ruger a little further away as a precaution. He didn't want a taste of what Cole had just received, and he could tell that Pam was in no mood to be messed with.

"That's fine by me, Pam," he said, fumbling for his cigarettes. "But it doesn't get us any closer to taking back the town. What are we gonna do, capture everyone and keep them tied up forever?"

Pam shook her head and gestured out the window. "Everyone else you can kill, Shep. Just not prisoners. That's the hill I'll die on. We start killing prisoners of war and we don't deserve to keep our country."

Shepherd lit his cigarette with a shaking hand, trying to settle his nerves and grab a little control over the situation. "OK," he agreed, blowing out a stream of smoke. "Now do you have any ideas as to how we're supposed to kill those guys out there?"

Ju-Won timidly raised a hand.

Pam smiled. "This isn't high school dear, you don't have to ask permission to speak."

Ju-Won cleared her throat and nodded. "Ummm... I think I have an idea."

•▼•

:::**20**:::

CHUNGJWA CHOI JUN-HO surveyed his internment camp with pride, and not a little frustration. Almost everything had gone to plan. *Almost* everything.

His key objectives had been achieved ahead of schedule. With the help of the firearms register the primary targets in Willow Falls had been successfully neutralized with only one Korean casualty, a young man who'd gone missing from his squad during an operation. The local citizenry had mostly been captured and interned, and most hadn't put up much of a fight.

In less than twenty four hours and using just a handful of men the town had been subdued. The shock and awe lightning strike had been a complete success, and the few prisoners who were spoiling for a fight as they were brought in had been deterred by a number of tactical executions. Choi had left the bodies where they fell, to serve as a warning to anyone who might be tempted to develop a taste for rebellion.

This attack, Choi thought, would be described in

military academies in the homeland for centuries hence. It was *textbook*. In just a day the most powerful nation on earth had been completely *decimated* by a vastly inferior force. The President had been assassinated, along with much of his high command. The nation's infrastructure had been disabled at the push of a button. The most serious threats, the heavily armed rednecks from which the US military traditionally drew its supply, had been captured or killed, neutralizing the risk of guerrilla warfare, while the cities had been left untouched. They would quickly destroy themselves without the Koreans lifting a finger. Hunger and disease would bring those hives of capitalist debauchery crashing down from within as their soft, weak denizens proved unable to survive without power.

The US was in chaos, ripe for conquest, and it had only taken a few thousand men placed at strategic points to bring it to its knees. Choi was proud that he could play a part, no matter how modest it may have been.

He had to admit that there had been a few... issues, however. Choi had begun his assault with three vehicles, the troop truck and two Humvees, and now he was down to just one. The truck had been stolen during the escape of a handful of prisoners, and on their way out of the park they'd rendered one of the Humvees inoperable. The second was out on a sweep of the suburbs, and it had been due to return almost an hour ago. Its occupants, three of Choi's most dependable soldiers and a capable female medic, had failed to answer radio calls.

Still, no matter. Choi's men were resourceful, and soon after losing the vehicles they'd collected a half dozen operational civilian vehicles from the town, all of them sturdy SUVs that would perform almost as well as a Humvee.

The setbacks had been troubling but minor, and they hadn't impacted on Choi's ability to describe the assault as a success. His superiors in Pyongyang would be proud of both his performance and his ability to adapt and react under pressure. This day's work must surely be enough to secure him his Soldier's Medal of Honor, First Class, an honor he'd secretly coveted for many years.

The *Chungjwa* pulled out his pocket watch and frowned at the time. The missing Humvee niggled at him like a loose tooth. The mission on which he'd sent his men should not have taxed them, and there should have been few enemies to face. It was a simple sweep of an already empty suburb, and even if they'd run into trouble they should have returned by now, or at least called in. He only hoped that the radio silence was a result of the EMP. Even shielded radios could struggle to transmit over long range in the aftermath, until the atmosphere righted itself. Maybe that's why they hadn't been able to make contact.

Ten more minutes. Ten more minutes and he'd order a few men to take the civilian vehicles to find them. He hoped it wouldn't be necessary. He had only a dozen men to guard several hundred civilian prisoners, and despite his confidence that the Americans wouldn't fight back he was reluctant to spread his forces any thinner. He knew that overconfidence could be fatal, and he'd been trained too well to rest on his laurels and assume that victory was assured.

Choi raised a hand to his temple, gingerly touching the angry, tender lump given to him by one of the prisoners as he'd escaped. That rankled him. He'd been left with the lump, a black eye and a split lip by the pilot, and his uniform had been torn and stained with his own blood during the assault. That would count against him when he faced his superiors. He'd already instructed his men to forget about the prisoners they'd lost – none of them would want to admit that they'd been bested by a group of civilians armed only with fireworks – but there would be no hiding the injuries, nor the deplorable state of his uniform. This was not... proper. It wasn't Choi's job to fight. An officer's job was to direct his men, not join them in the fray, and he'd have a hard time explaining why he'd...

Choi turned towards Willow Falls and narrowed

his eyes. At the edge of the suburbs a column of dust rose into the air, and in the distance he heard the sound of an engine. *Finally!* Relief swept over him as the Humvee emerged from the trees that lined the road beyond the park. Finally it was all coming together. The men had returned to strengthen his numbers and help guard the prisoners. The Humvee could be added to the civilian vehicles and soften at least some of the embarrassment Choi felt at losing the other two. It would all be OK. There would be no more humiliation. Maybe when his superiors finally arrived there would be no need to even tell them about the lost vehicles. Maybe it would be enough to simply arrive in the Humvee and pretend his forces were at full strength.

The vehicle finally turned into the parking lot at the edge of the park, kicking up yet more dust as it barreled across the rough surface. Now it was close enough that Choi could see through the windshield. The young medic, Park Ju-Won, sat behind the wheel. He couldn't see *Daewi* Jeong Hwan or the other men, but perhaps they were...

Something was wrong. The Humvee wasn't slowing down.

Choi Jun-Ho felt the hairs stand up on the back of his neck. The vehicle was picking up speed as it approached, tearing across the park when it should be drawing to a halt. He quickly scanned his eyes around the park and saw that none of his men were paying attention. They barely seem to have noticed the return of the vehicle, and nobody seemed concerned at its speed.

He didn't want to yell out. Despite his misgivings he didn't dare show himself up in front of his men. He could already taste the shame and embarrassment he'd feel if he sounded the alarm only for the Humvee to pull to a stop beside him. He felt rooted to the spot. He wanted to move. He was desperate to run for the cover of the nearby trees, but again the shame would be too much if he—

And then he saw it. Through the windshield of the vehicle he saw the hatred in Ju-Won's eyes.

In an instant his years of physical training kicked in, his muscles reacting without the dull, lumpen input of his conscious mind that would only slow his reaction time. As the Humvee barreled forward he sprang to the side, falling onto his rolled shoulder, clearing the path of the vehicle just as it plowed over the spot he'd been standing just a moment ago. He felt the heat of the engine against his skin.

Choi reached for his sidearm before he'd come to a stop, slipping it from its holster with one hand as he steadied himself on the ground with the other. Still he was operating on autopilot, relying on his training as he aimed his service revolver at the back of the speeding Humvee. In just a few seconds he emptied it into the vehicle, the bullets striking the armor plating like bugs on a windshield.

Finally his men noticed what was happening, but it was too late. Before the first could draw his weapon the Humvee crashed into the barrier blocking the entrance to the barbed wire enclosure, bursting it open and crushing an inattentive guard as it went. It skidded to a halt just short of the American prisoners, and as Choi reloaded the Americans began to flock towards the vehicle with murder in their eyes.

Choi had no earthly clue what was happening, nor why, but he knew one thing for certain. He knew what the Americans would do next.

They'd noticed that the person inside the Humvee was not their rescuer, but their captor.

•▼•

:::21:::

JU-WON PRAYED AS the American prisoners began to surround the Humvee. The first few approached cautiously, unsure what was happening, but their courage grew as they noticed the terror in the eyes of the young woman sitting behind the wheel. As word spread back through the crowd they pressed in closer around the vehicle, those at the back pushing the people in front forward, eager for a look. A brave soul banged on Ju-Won's door and within moments more joined in, slapping and punching the doors and windows with their fists, no doubt assuming that she'd driven into the enclosure by accident.

She knew they couldn't hope to break through the ballistic glass or so much as leave a scratch in the armored doors, but she knew she couldn't stay in there forever. If the plan was going to work she'd have to climb out and face the angry rabble.

"OK, honey, you just sit tight and let me deal with this." Pam awkwardly raised herself from her hiding place on the back seat. Immediately Ju-Won saw the confusion in the faces of the Americans surrounding the vehicle, but a moment later the anger returned.

"Those bastards have Pam!" Ju-Won couldn't see the man who yelled it out, but as soon as he did the crowd pressed in even closer, all of them determined to rescue their friend and tear Ju-Won limb from limb.

"Please don't let them kill me," Ju-Won pleaded, her voice weak with fear.

"Don't worry, hon," Pam replied, though now her voice sounded less assured. "Maybe duck down under your seat, though. This may get a little crazy."

Ju-Won shuffled down as low as she could as Pam unlocked the rear door and pushed it open, struggling against the weight of the people pressed against it. Immediately the roar of the crowd around the vehicle grew to fever pitch. Pam opened her mouth and began to speak, but before she got out so much as a word she found herself pulled from the back of the truck, vanishing into a sea of people eager to whisk her to safety. She fought against it, tried to protest, but it was as useless as swimming against a rip tide. The sea of humanity outside the truck swallowed her up, and in her place... in her place came the men. They fought each other to be the first through the open door, each of them eager to get their pound of flesh.

Ju-Won screamed as someone reached over the rear seat, grabbed a fistful of her long hair and yanked hard. She felt hands close around her arms and reach down to her legs, tugging her forcefully from the seat and dragging her into the back of the Humvee. She tried to fight back but she could barely move an inch against the weight of the hands pressing her down.

Someone grabbed hold of her jacket and pulled, tearing open her fatigues. Another hand pressed down on her neck, and another clamped over her mouth. The weight on her was immense, a writhing mass of people each desperate to exact their revenge on one of their captors. Someone punched her in the gut, driving the air from her lungs, and she couldn't take another breath. Another punch came, and another, and colored spots began to flash before her eyes as her lungs cried out for air.

So this is how I'm going to die. The thought came to her matter-of-factly, a calm voice speaking in her head as if it were watching what was happening from a distance. Ju-Won felt as if her ribs were breaking beneath the weight of the people crushing her, but the voice remained calm even as the pain made her want to scream. *It will all be over soon. This pain will pass. Let yourself go.*

Another punch in the gut, and one in the face. Two strong hands grabbed at her feet now, dragging her out from the Humvee, onto the grass and into the crowd. She kept her eyes squeezed tight, praying that they'd end it quickly and without too much more pain. She tried to roll into a ball, but the hands held her feet firm and kept dragging her further from the vehicle. Suddenly the weight returned. There were people on her once again, crushing her against the ground.

"Alright, you God damn animals, *that's enough!*"

Another punch in the face. Ju-Won's ears rang with the pain and shock.

"You get the hell off of her this second, Boyd Gibson, or you'll feel my foot up your ass!"

Ju-Won felt a weight lift suddenly from her body. She slowly opened her eyes, her vision blurred by the tears streaming down her cheeks. A large figure loomed over her, pushing people back, guarding her like a lioness with her cub. It was Pam.

"That's better," she said, as the crowd began to settle. She pointed down to Ju-Won. "Now this girl saved my life, and she's trying to save yours. Leave her be. The enemy's out there. Are we all on the same page?" She looked around at the crowd, meeting their eyes as she scanned. "Good. Now here's what we're—"

Ju-Won didn't hear the shot. She could barely see through the tears and she was focused on gulping oxygen into her lungs, but she saw the blood begin to spread across Pam's Stars and Stripes apron. She saw Pam drop to her knees, a shocked expression on her face.

And then the floodgates burst.

The Korean soldiers outside the enclosure had been taken entirely by surprise. They weren't expecting an attack, and when the *Chungjwa* had opened fire on the returning Humvee they couldn't make sense of it. They could see that inside the vehicle was Park Ju-Won, their medic, and nobody wanted to be the first to join the *Chungjwa* in firing on her.

It was only when their leader reloaded his weapon and climbed on top of the burned out Humvee that they began to realize this wasn't an error. This wasn't a case of mistaken identity or confusion. The Chungjwa could clearly see Ju-Won as she was pulled from the vehicle, and he still leveled his revolver in her direction. When he pulled the trigger and struck the large woman in the American flag apron they knew what to do. His revolver was – quite literally – the starter pistol.

As one they raised their rifles, and they opened fire on the Americans.

Around Ju-Won chaos reigned. Her countrymen fired wildly on the crowd, a dozen rifles emptying into a mass of bodies. Around her people fled for cover that wasn't there, desperately trying to escape the edge of the crowd and reach the relative safety of the center. Men, women and children screamed as people fell to the grass, wounded or killed, and in the middle of them all Ju-Won dragged herself through the forest of legs to reach Pam, lying on her back and clutching her side.

"Are you OK?" Ju-Won pulled Pam's hand away to inspect her wound.

Pam tried to smile reassuringly, but it came out as a pained grimace. "Just knocked the wind out of me, darling, that's all," she wheezed, closing her hand once more across what Ju-Won saw was only a nasty flesh wound. The bullet had passed straight through her side and out the back, thankfully passing through a layer of fat rather than anything vital. "Go on now," she said, pushing Ju-Won away with a bloodied hand, "you have a job to do."

Ju-Won nodded. She wished she didn't. Around her the gunfire continued to erupt, and as Americans fell or fled the crowd thinned, exposing her more by the second to the path of a bullet. She looked up to the open rear door of the Humvee. It was just twenty yards away, but twenty yards through a firefight may as well be a mile.

There was nothing for it. If she stayed where she was she'd be dead in minutes, and every last American with her. There was only once chance to survive. With a final squeeze of Pam's shoulder Ju-Won pushed herself from the ground, lifting herself from the cover of the thinning crowd, and sprinted towards the rear of the Humvee.

As soon as she exposed herself the soldiers began to target her, peppering the ground around her with the kicked up turf of near misses. As she ran she felt the air disturbed as bullets whizzed by her, missing her by the slightest breath. When she was within touching distance of the Humvee she threw herself forward towards the safety of the rear seat, covering the final yard in mid air.

The shot caught her in the thigh, a ricochet from the armored plating. She barely felt it, just a sudden pinch in the skin as she crashed down onto the rear seat, but the moment she looked down and saw the blood the pain flooded in. She gasped with agony as she tore open her fatigue pants, and at the sight of the wound she felt hot vomit climb up her throat. No exit wound, but it was only a glancing shot, tearing a three inch line across the skin of her thigh. The bullet fragment was still visible, a glistening shard hidden beneath a bright pulse of blood at the end of a long, scored gash.

No time to worry about it now. More were dying by the second. She swallowed the searing bile and pushed the pain deep. She forced herself to climb up and over the rear seat and into the trunk, dragging her injured leg behind her, to the pile stacked there like a bundle of kindling.

Guns. Lots of them.

On the far side of the Humvee two dozen

Americans hid from the assault, mothers and fathers holding their children close. There wasn't enough room for them all, and those on the edges desperately fought to push their children deeper behind cover even as they exposed themselves to the gunfire. Ju-Won grabbed an armful of rifles, muttered a silent prayer and kicked open the door, hoping against hope that they'd heed Pam's word that she was a friend.

"Guys!" Despite the pain and terror she remembered not to let her acquired American accent slip to her native Korean. "Fight back! They're loaded!"

She dropped the bundle of rifles into the crowd and reached back into the trunk for more, and when she returned she found that every man behind the Humvee had taken up arms. With the second bundle the women helped themselves, and by the time she returned with the third even some of the older children held weapons.

The Americans were suddenly transformed. No longer were they meek and terrified prisoners cowering in fear from the gunfire. With the weight of the weapons in their hands they found the confidence to stand.

The moment they reached their feet and drew up their rifles the fate of the soldiers was sealed.

•▼•

:::22:::

SHEPHERD STAMPED THE gas pedal into the carpet as he tore across the gravel parking lot, pushing the wheezing Jeep to its limit. Ju-Won had asked him to follow five minutes behind her, to hang back until she had the chance to break through to the prisoners and distribute the weapons, but when he'd heard the gunfire in the distance before he'd counted out three minutes he'd lost patience.

The park was almost unrecognizable since he'd last seen it the day before, a war zone in what had been a peaceful meadow. The first thing Shepherd noticed was the burned out shell of a Humvee, its windows blown out and tires deflated. Fifty yards ahead of the charred wreck, at the center of the park right where every July Fourth the townsfolk played a friendly game of touch football while countless burgers sizzled away on their grills, a coiled, twisted mass of barbed wire penned off a wide patch of grass. Ju-Won's Humvee sat in the center of the enclosure, and around it a crowd of several hundred Americans scattered like headless chickens as Korean troops fired into the mass. Even at this distance Shepherd could see bodies on the ground, and he swallowed a lump in his throat as he realized that some of them were probably his friends.

He could also see that the people trapped in the enclosure were fighting back, and they were winning. Already four Korean soldiers were on the ground, three dead and one writhing in agony, and the rest were scattering now they realized this wasn't a one-sided fight. Five of them had fled the gunfire for the safety of the burned out Humvee, cowering behind the armor plating and firing blindly into the crowd whenever they dared expose themselves for a moment. Shepherd knew they'd be safe back there, protected by the thick armor and able to continue their assault on the Americans as long as their ammo held out.

No, he thought, pointing the Jeep in the direction of the Humvee. *Not one more drop of American blood will be spilled today.* He shifted down and stamped even harder on the gas, setting himself on a collision course with the wreck.

To the left of him he saw that Big Joe had the same idea. His truck bounced across the park towards the remaining three soldiers, all of them attempting to flee into the trees. They didn't get far once Cole and the chief got them in their sights. One by one they dropped to the ground.

The soldiers by the Humvee didn't appear to hear

Shepherd coming. They were too focused on firing into the crowd to notice the roar of the Jeep behind them, and as Shepherd barreled towards them he squeezed the wheel so hard his knuckles whitened. He stepped on the brake as he hit the first soldier, an instinctive reaction any driver would have as they plowed into someone, but it was too late to make any difference to his speed. The Jeep slammed into the side of the burned out Humvee at an angle, scraping along the armor from back to front, and all five of the soldiers vanished beneath the hood in the blink of an eye.

The final man had just enough time to turn his head before he was struck. He seemed to meet Shepherd's eyes with a look of disbelief and horror, just long enough to realize his mistake, and an instant later he performed his final act as a speed hump beneath the tires of the Jeep.

Shepherd felt himself thrown forward, straining against his seat belt as his truck came to a jarring halt against the side of the Humvee. The wind was knocked out of him, his ribs crushed by the belt. The screech of steel on steel battered his ears and he felt like he'd been hit full in the face by a freight train, but as he slumped back into his seat and caught his breath he could tell he'd done himself no serious harm. He'd be aching for a week, but there were no broken bones.

The Jeep was a different story altogether. Steam billowed from the radiator and fuel sprayed on the shattered windshield from the severed end of a hose. At the back of Shepherd's throat his ragged breath caught on a fog of thick, acrid smoke creeping through the vents that told him something in the engine bay was on fire, and spreading fast.

In just a few moments the stink of burning rubber and oil filled the truck, and Shepherd flinched as the fuel on the hood caught fire, bursting a black-edged plume against the windshield with a soft *whumph*. He clawed at his seat belt and scrambled towards the passenger door, the only way out now the driver's door was crushed against the Humvee beside it.

The smoke stung his eyes. Through pinprick tears he could see the flames licking from the hood, and he felt the panic rise as he blindly reached out for the door handle and found it stuck, the door buckled shut by the crash. He could feel the stifling heat of the fire reach out to him through the air vents in the dash, but he managed to keep his head long enough to shuffle into the passenger seat, brace against the roof and bring his boots up to the side window.

Three firm kicks was all it took to shatter the glass. Clean, cool air rushed into the cab and Shepherd scrambled towards the broken window, sliding painfully over the sharp edges in the frame, falling face first to the grass and taking deep, gulping breaths to clear his seared lungs of the burning smoke.

He was still on all fours, struggling to take a breath without gagging, when he felt the pistol pressed against the back of his head.

•▾•

:::**23**:::

CHUNGJWA CHOI JUN-HO could barely believe his misfortune. Just minutes ago everything seemed to be coming together. He'd had the town subdued and the prisoners cowering in fear. The beachhead was secured, and with hundreds of human shields at his mercy nobody would have ever dared risk an assault as he waited for reinforcements to arrive.

Now... now it was all up in smoke. That traitorous *bitch* had armed the Americans and stolen away his fire superiority, and the world had collapsed around him with frightening speed.

Treachery was the one thing he hadn't planned for; the one thing he hadn't even *considered*. In an army built on a foundation of total, unquestioning obedience it had never occurred to Choi that someone like Ju-Won might betray her own people.

She'd pay for this, and Choi would make sure the price was unbearably steep. He'd stand over her as she took her final breath, but not before showing her what happened to people who turned against the People's Republic. She'd watch her entire family die screaming in agony, and only when he'd seen the spark fade from her eyes, only once he'd utterly destroyed her world and slaughtered her very spirit, would he grant her death. The last thing she'd see would be the sole of his boot as he crushed her into the ground.

But first... first he had to escape this nightmare. As the Americans began to return fire he'd taken shelter beneath the burned out Humvee, but now the prisoners were escaping from their enclosure he knew he couldn't remain hidden. Before long they'd find him. They'd drag him out from his hiding place and exact their revenge. He knew he'd have to find some way out of the park, and he knew there was no chance he could slip away unseen to the tree line.

He also knew he had just one final bullet. It was the bullet he kept in his breast pocket, his most terrible insurance policy. Choi's orders had been clear, and his final order had been the clearest of all. He knew too much to be taken by the enemy, and if capture ever seemed certain he was to do what was necessary to avoid interrogation. Those were the exact words his superiors had used. *Do what is necessary.*

Choi had believed he could follow that order without a second thought. He'd told himself that his sacrifice, should it become necessary, would be an honorable death. A fitting tribute to the fatherland and, as a famed American leader had once put it, the last full measure of devotion. He'd prayed he'd never have to use that final bullet, but he'd never doubted that he'd pull the trigger without hesitation should the time come.

But now... now the enemy was closing in, and suicide was the last thing on his mind. He wanted to *live*. He wanted to fight back, to have his revenge against those who'd stolen victory from him even as he'd felt its weight resting on his fingertips. He didn't want to meekly accept defeat. He wanted to rage against the dying of the light.

On the far side of the enclosure the truck that had chased down and viciously slaughtered the last of his men turned and began to roar back towards the Humvee, no doubt coming to the aid of its driver. Choi knew he had only seconds to act. In a few moments he'd be trapped, and he'd—

Above him he heard the sound of shattering glass. He turned away from the approaching truck in time to see a figure fall from the crashed Jeep, tumbling to the ground like a rag doll. A man, gasping and choking for air but very much alive.

This was his chance.

Choi shuffled awkwardly on hands and knees to the back of the Humvee, pulling himself to his feet out of sight of the approaching truck. He crept silently around the burning Jeep, careful not to give away his presence as the man coughed and spluttered, struggling to breathe after escaping the burning Jeep. The American was clearly larger and stronger than Choi, but it appeared he was unarmed. Choi had his revolver, and he chambered his last remaining bullet.

"Stand up," he ordered, pressing the gun firmly against the base of the man's skull.

He wouldn't need more than one bullet.

•▼•

:::24:::

SHEPHERD HAD NO idea where the soldier had come from. He'd been certain he'd killed them all in the crash. Even if one of them had somehow survived he couldn't possibly still be standing so soon after being introduced to the steel bull bars at the front of the Jeep, but as he stood and turned to meet his attacker it became clear this wasn't one of the men he'd hit. This man had taken a beating, but he hadn't been under the wheels of a truck.

Shepherd wanted nothing more than to lay down and catch his breath, but his captor had other ideas. He slowly maneuvered himself behind Shepherd, pressing the gun against his ear as Big Joe's truck approached, and with Shepherd as a shield he started slowly walking backwards towards the tree line.

"If you give yourself up I'll make sure they go easy on you," Shepherd croaked, his throat bone dry. "We'll hand you over to the authorities as soon as they arrive. You'll get a fair trial and everything. Just put down the gun and surrender. It's over."

Choi laughed bitterly. "Nobody is coming to help you, American," he said, pressing the gun harder against Shepherd's head. "You're all alone. My people have killed your leaders and burned your country to the ground, and soon more will arrive to deal with the rest of you."

Shepherd's rebellious streak kicked in, compelling him to to stand firm and anchor his feet, stopping Choi in his tracks. Despite the gun against his head he couldn't allow himself to be led backwards. "You think we'll give up just because you killed our leaders?" He half turned towards his captor and shook his head in disbelief. "Jesus, you really don't know us at all, do you? We got plenty of guys who can wear a suit and kiss babies. You want to kill our leaders? We'll take a half day next Tuesday and elect new ones, and when they bomb the crap out of your capital we'll throw them a damned ticker tape parade."

Choi tried to pull him back, but Shepherd dug his heels in. Twenty yards away Big Joe pulled his truck to a halt beside the burned out Humvee, and Cole and the chief climbed out with their weapons raised.

Shepherd continued. "You really don't get it. There's no victory waiting for you at the end of this. There's no throne waiting for your fat ass bowl cut boss. You don't get to conquer America. You can't. You can take every scrap of land from Yankee Stadium to the Golden Gate Bridge, but you still won't have conquered us. America isn't just a country. It's not just land and a flag. It's a Goddamned spar-spangled idea, and it's bigger than all of us. As long as a single one of us still believes in it we won't rest until every last one of you gets the ass kicking you richly deserve." He fully turned towards Choi, still pressing the gun against his head, and he met his eyes. "And I'll be first in line. This is your last chance. Put down the gun, or these folks'll shoot you where it takes a week to die."

•▼•

:::25:::

FOR A MOMENT Choi was frozen to the spot. He stared at Shepherd in disbelief, amazed that the man would look down the barrel of a revolver without a hint of fear in his eyes. This wasn't how he was supposed to react. He should be quaking with terror at the prospect of death. He should be happy to act as Choi's shield to earn himself a slim chance of survival.

Choi had never intended to shoot the man. He knew that to use his final bullet on the American would only hasten his own death, but the hostage had left him with little choice. If he failed to pull the trigger now the spell would be broken, and his power lost. He would be defeated, quickly overpowered by—

The blow came out of nowhere. Choi didn't even see the American move before the jab caught him on the bridge of his nose, rocking his head back as if it was on a spring. He stumbled back, stunned, and felt a quick right hook catch him painfully on the chin. In a daze he struggled to keep his feet, and a moment later he felt a steadying hand around his wrist. The American was trying to take his revolver.

Desperation drove Choi to fight back. He snatched

the gun back and swung blindly with his free hand, catching the man with a glancing blow to the shoulder, but his clenched fist landed like a soft breeze. It had been years since Choi had trained in hand to hand combat, and years since he'd so much as thrown a punch. His brand of discipline was administered through the barrel of a gun, and it was only now that he realized his physical skills had lost their edge.

Through blurred, tearful eyes he saw the American carefully advance on him, wary of the weapon still clutched in his hands. Choi raised the pistol, waving it before him like a talisman but unable to focus enough to trust his aim. It was all he could do to make sure he kept the American between himself and the armed men, blocking them from taking a shot.

The man lunged forward, a roar erupting from his throat.

•▼•

:::26:::

SHEPHERD BARRELLED INTO the soldier at a run, dipping his shoulder to duck under the pointed gun. He knew he needed to end this quickly, before the dazed officer could manage to get off a shot.

The two men tumbled to the ground, wrestling over the steel clutched in the Korean's hand. Shepherd tried to pry it from his fingers but the man held it in a death grip, clinging onto the revolver for dear life.

Rolling onto his shoulder for leverage, Shepherd thrust violently forward with his forehead, crushing the officer's nose against his face with a gruesome crunch of shattered cartilage. As he pulled back he felt the man's hot blood on his face, and beneath him the soldier weakened. His hand began to loosen on the gun held against his thigh, and Shepherd reached for it once more. He grabbed at the soldier's fingers and bent them back, prying them away from the grip, but his opponent wasn't yet ready to submit. He yanked the weapon back, trying desperately with the last of his strength to take control once more. He squeezed his fingers around the grip once more.

The shot echoed across the park.

Shepherd froze. Adrenaline coursed through his veins and his heartbeat thumped in his ears, and in his frantic state he couldn't tell if he was hit. He'd felt the jolt of the shot but there was no pain, but then he could barely feel pain anywhere. He looked down towards the gun, and as he saw the crimson blood seep across his shirt he felt the icy grip of fear in his heart.

And then the officer began to wail.

Shepherd rolled to the side, pulling the revolver from the man's unresisting hands, and he saw what had happened. A small hole was punched through the olive green camouflage of the soldier's jacket, and around it a patch of blood slowly crept out in a glistening halo. It looked as if the bullet had hit his stomach, just beneath his navel.

Shepherd almost felt pity for the man, lying there wounded and defeated, a broken creature alone among the enemy. That pity quickly burned away like a morning mist as he remembered the American bodies that lay just a short distance away, but still it was enough to decide to give the man a quick and easy death.

He took hold of the revolver and brought it to the man's temple, and without ceremony squeezed the trigger.

The hammer clicked, but the shot didn't come. He

squeezed, and again, and then once more. Each time the hammer came down on an empty chamber. With a sigh he pushed out the cylinder and tipped the bullets into his palm. All spent.

Oh well, he thought. At least he'd tried. With a wheeze and a stab in his ribs he pulled himself from the ground. Now the pain was returning, and it came from everywhere. He looked through stinging, bloodshot eyes at the crowd gathered around. The chief took a hesitant step forward, a shotgun resting in the crook of his arm.

"Umm... what do you think we should do with him, Shep?"

Shepherd looked down at the Korean bleeding out on the grass, and down at the spent revolver in his hand. He tossed the gun to the ground and shrugged.

"It's your call, Chief, but I'd say let God deal with him."

He took a step in the direction of Ju Won's Humvee, desperate to get back to town and find a bottle of bourbon to take the edge off the pain. As he walked the silent crowd parted to let him through, and as he passed it closed behind him.

He didn't look back as they began to gather around the Korean, and he paid no attention as he heard the first blows rain down.

•▼•

:::27:::

SHEPHERD SAT ALONE and silent in his favorite booth, the one with a long, jagged tear in the red vinyl bench seat. He'd made that tear with a clumsy boot heel years earlier, and he'd patched it himself after Pam threatened to cut off his pancake supply. Now he idly picked at the frayed edge of the patch, his mind wandering and a cigarette burning unnoticed down to its butt on the edge of the plate in front of him.

He wanted nothing more than to sleep, but he was far too wired. The adrenaline still coursed through his system, and all he could do was sit and wait until he finally crashed. Besides, Ju-Won was in the kitchen stitching Pam's wound, and hidden from the townsfolk in the walk in freezer the two Korean soldiers lay bound and gagged. He'd promised Ju-Won he wouldn't leave until they could figure out how to deal with them.

Through the open door of the diner came the occasional cheer from the crowd out in the square.

Before leaving the park Big Joe had rescued the shortwave radio from the wreck of Shepherd's truck, and he'd hooked an aerial extension over the branches of the willow tree to boost its range. What seemed like the whole town was out there listening to the news coming in from around the country.

In the aftermath of the EMP, the announcers reported, the people of the nation had mobilized. They'd set about repairing old battery powered ham radios and tapping into shielded NOAA radio towers in an attempt to restore some measure of communication. Many towns had even sent out 'Reveres', riders and drivers spreading news from town to town by word of mouth, a method that was proving surprisingly successful. News updates were passed along like an enormous game of Telephone and the reports were being re-broadcast from stations in Canada and Mexico, beyond the range of the attack. They told of a nation that was down but far from out; a nation that had taken a kicking, but had immediately kicked back twice as hard.

Willow Falls was far from alone. All across the country North Korean ground forces had struck, in at least twenty states and hundreds of towns. Most of the cells were little more than a dozen or so strong, nimble and fast moving forces multiplied by their tactical preparedness and working vehicles. They'd hit hard and fast, playing on the chaos and confusion that reigned in the hours after the lights had flickered out, and they'd caused immense loss of life that belied their small numbers.

The radio announcers speculated that these cells had been intended as an advance force, their objective to dig themselves in like ticks, surround themselves with American hostages and use them as leverage, allowing reinforcements to enter the country unmolested. Already several container ships and aircraft large and small had been spotted heading for the US, ferrying troops and military commanders to the front line. The plan, it seemed, had been to occupy and colonize.

But the plan had failed. The North Koreans had sorely misjudged their enemy, and across the nation the invaders had been fought to a standstill. From the orange groves of California to the cornfields of Iowa to the forests of Maine, the Koreans had learned that, unlike their own people, Americans don't kneel.

All across the country the invaders had been caught on the back foot. They hadn't been prepared for the ferocity of the Americans, nor their willingness to lay down their lives for each other. In Union Springs, Alabama a chemistry teacher had surrendered himself to the invaders as they launched an assault on hundreds of kids hiding out in the local high school gym, only to blow himself and his attackers to kingdom come with a bomb he'd constructed using chemicals from his supply closet. In Winchester, Kentucky a civil war reenactment society had led an assault on a heavily armed cell using nothing but muskets and lead shot, taking the Koreans out to the last man. There were even rumors that somewhere in Florida the manager of a reptile farm had released hundreds of venomous snakes into a Walmart store a Korean unit was using as a base of operations.

The Koreans were fleeing, panicked and defeated, and the atmosphere out in the square was electric with cheering and laughter erupting every few minutes as new reports flooded in over the airwaves. The liquor and beer flowed from private supplies stockpiled in advance of the July 4th celebrations, and if you squinted your eyes and forgot that there were bodies still waiting to be buried out in the park you could almost imagine that this was just a regular day.

The sun was about to set, casting long shadows across the square and promising the blissful cool of a Virginia summer evening. Rich, sweet pipe smoke drifted on the air, a cloud billowing above a huddle of elderly men who'd dragged their rockers out to the base of the willow tree. The squeals and laughter of children, blissfully oblivious to the events of the day, rang out across the square, and above it all the triumphant calls emerged from the radio, telling a story of a victorious America that had once again beaten back an invading enemy; that had one more declared its hard fought independence. The Korean forces within the country were being mopped up. The container ships on the way to the coasts were being stopped and boarded, and the planes in the air were being forced down or shot down, depending on how readily their pilots cooperated.

Shepherd squeezed the bridge of his nose between his fingers, stubbed out his smoldering cigarette and slid slowly from the booth, stretching stiffly to relieve the pain of his aching joints. He wished he could join the townsfolk in their celebrations. He wished he could crack open a beer and rejoice, but he knew better. He knew the nightmare wasn't over. He knew it was only just beginning, and what's more he suspected that most of the crowd out in the square knew it too.

There was an edge to their laughter, barely noticeable but clear as a bell if you were listening for it. It was a laughter that betrayed a panicked desperation; a collective denial that said 'I don't want to be the first to break this spell.' They knew all too well that the power wasn't coming back anytime soon, and they knew that soon enough they'd have to face up to what that meant. Not just yet, though. Not tonight. One more beer wouldn't hurt.

Shepherd made his way out of the diner and into the thronged crowd, wincing with pain as invisible hands slapped him on the back and unseen voices congratulated him for 'takin' out those damned Gooks.' A young man, the manager of the local bait store, handed him a beer, but he pushed it away with a grateful smile.

"Hey, Shep. *Shep!*" Shepherd looked around for the source of the cry, and eventually spotted Big Joe hunkered down by the shortwave. "Get your butt over here. Hey, everyone! Stop your yapping and listen to this."

Shepherd lowered himself painfully to the ground beside Joe, a space clearing around him as he sat, and Joe nudged the volume knob higher as the announcer's voice returned.

... sworn in during a hurried ceremony yesterday in Madrid. President Wells immediately appointed William Kelley, his former chief aide at the Department of Commerce, as his Vice President, but it's understood he won't be making any more cabinet level appointments until the situation is more stable.

In a brief speech delivered today on the deck of the USS Dwight D. Eisenhower, President Wells gave his thanks to the governments of the world for their offers of aid to the US. He promised swift and harsh reprisals against North Korea in response to their attack, and pledged to restore the United States to its place as a shining beacon of hope in an often dark and hopeless world. However, his words may be of little comfort to those millions of Americans still trapped without power.

The announcer's voice was replaced with that of President Wells, a slightly nasal and hesitant drone. The stress in his voice carried clearly over thousands of miles, and it was obvious that this former Acting Secretary of Commerce was not accustomed to speaking to a crowd.

The years ahead will be, we should make no mistake, a long and desperate struggle. Our allies around the world have pledged to do everything in their power to help restore our great nation to its former glory, but we must accept that this goal may not be reached in our lifetime. I believe that it would be wrong to... uh, to comfort ourselves with false hope and unrealistic expectations. I believe... I believe in honesty, and in... I believe I should be honest. I think that's best for everyone.

I also believe that Americans are up to the challenge. Even though it may be several years before power is restored to the United States I believe that if we all work together and... if we work as a team I believe we'll, uh, find a strength we never knew we possessed. I... let's get to work. Let's... let's go get 'em.

The voice faded out, and a moment later the announcer returned.

President Wells immediately drew criticism from

many for the overly pessimistic tone of his message to America. Citizens overseas complained that his words have done little but stoke fears at home that no end to this crisis is in sight. Indeed, early reports have emerged of a wave of looting and civil unrest in several cities, including violence at a FEMA camp on Long Island that resulted in multiple deaths.

"Did he really say years?"

Shepherd turned towards the voice, and as he did he felt his heart sink. It was the manager of the bait store, a man who just a minute ago had tried to hand him a beer. Now his fingers closed tight around the six pack in his hands. Others around him also seemed suddenly guarded, their smiles fading as they realized that generosity might not be the best option.

"Well now," Shepherd stammered, silently cursing the new President, "I guess he's talking about full coverage, right? I mean, it could take us a few years to get all the big transformers installed and restore power to every home, but it might just be a few weeks before we get things started. They got all sorts of things these days. Wind, solar... and you just know that Tesla guy has a few tricks up his sleeve. I don't think we need to worry too much."

Even Shepherd wasn't convinced by his own words. He'd heard the same speech as everyone else, and he knew there was no way to spin it into a positive. It would take years. Years without refrigeration to store food. Without the power needed to properly farm anything larger than a vegetable patch. Without the power to operate gas pumps, sanitize water, or run the lights in an operating room.

Their future would be spent in darkness.

Already Shepherd could see people peeling away at the edge of the crowd, heading at a fast walk back to their homes. As he watched he saw the cheerful crowd draw in on itself, wives moving closer to their husbands, pulling their kids in tight.

A woman called out to her little girl sitting on a hydrant by the door of Pam's diner. "Come on now, Sarah, we gotta get home." By the diner the girl was sharing a bag of potato chips with a little boy with tousled red hair, and as she turned to her mother the boy snatched the bag from her hands with an impish grin.

"You give that back, Dylan Greene! You give it back to her right now!"

The little boy froze at the order, shocked by the anger in the woman's voice. His lower lip trembled, and a moment later the tears began to flow. He dropped the bag of chips to the ground and a mournful wail called out across the square. Another woman rushed towards him and swept him up in her arms, but not before picking up the chips and shoving the bag in her pocket.

"Those are Dylan's chips, Val! He was nice enough

to share them with your girl. How dare you upset him like that?"

"Like hell they are! You know damned well we brought those from home. Now hand them back to Sarah, or so help me I'll give your boy something to cry about."

Shepherd shook his head sadly, turning away from the row and pushing his way back through the dispersing crowd towards the diner. He didn't want to hear any more of this, not after the day he'd had. Five minutes ago the town was united, celebrating its victory, and now people were fighting in the street over half a bag of barbecue Lays.

As he stepped through the door of the diner he heard a ruckus from the kitchen, and a moment later a few men emerged with their arms full of grease paper wrapped hamburger patties. They shoved past him and vanished into the street, and a moment later Pam pushed her way slowly through the swinging doors from the kitchen. She was almost bent double, her shirt stained with blood and clearly in pain. Behind her Ju-Won fussed over her, trying and failing to support Pam's weight.

"What the hell's going on, Shep? Did you see what they did?" She leaned against the counter, her breath ragged and her face red. "Assholes just helped themselves to the last of the food! What the heck's happening?"

Shepherd slumped back into his favorite booth, suddenly exhausted beyond belief. He barely had the energy to speak. "It's just the world going to Hell, Pam," he sighed. "Come on, sit with me." He gestured to the bench seat opposite, and with great difficulty Ju-Won helped her over and lowered her down.

Shepherd knew he couldn't keep his eyes open much longer. The adrenaline was finally spent, and he could feel his body succumbing to sleep even as he struggle to stay awake. "Would you mind praying with me, Pam?" he asked. He didn't know why. After what had happened he struggled to believe there was anyone watching over them.

Nonetheless Pam took his hand across the table, a moment later joined by Ju-Won's, and together they whispered a quiet prayer. For food. For power. For the world, just for a moment, to make sense again.

Shepherd drifted off before they were finished. His hand fell limp from Pam's, and his body melted into the soft foam padding of the bench seat as his head fell back against the vinyl.

Before he slept the last thing he heard, far in the distance but approaching fast, was gunfire.

•Y•

THE SERIES CONCLUDES

WITH

AMERICA STRONG

Made in United States
Troutdale, OR
04/23/2024

19381067R00130